T0195677

Untold Stories, Him & Her

Raw and Unapologetic

WAYNE DEAN

authorHOUSE

AuthorHouse™
1663 Liberty Drive
Bloomington, IN 47403
www.authorhouse.com
Phone: 833-262-8899

Published by AuthorHouse 02/26/2022

ISBN: 978-1-6655-3581-6 (sc)
ISBN: 978-1-6655-3580-9 (hc)
ISBN: 978-1-6655-3586-1 (e)

Library of Congress Control Number: 2021917396

Dedication

This book is dedicated to the men and women whose
patience, understanding, and sincerity
reflects their hearts.

Contents

Introduction

If they claim that men are from Mars and women from Venus, then I am inclined to ask about the origins of male and female babies who eventually become adults. Though the expression is strictly hypothetical; it nevertheless draws a distinction between the two genders that strangely brings them together as mutually supportive of each other in the extension of human existence. This natural attraction is in harmony with the universal laws of nature. Being from separate places may be the glue to their union. Like a magnet that has a north and a south pole, the opposite pole attracts. The north pole will attract the south pole and vice versa. If they are placed with north to north or south to south, they will repel. A natural attraction to the opposite sex represents the north and the south.

Our behavior is naturally telling of a distinct gender. Women talk about clothing, sales, relationships, cooking, physical appearance, and men. Men talk about money, cars, politics, work, sports, and women. The common denominator is obvious.

A woman will get very emotional over a simple issue, while a man will wonder what's her problem. A woman will pay attention to the finer details, while a man will look at the overall picture. He will shop for clothing in less than thirty minutes while she will shop a whole day. Most people expect that their partner will be similar in their attitudes, perceptions, behavior, and values but the answer is revealed in the degree to which these thoughts and actions are played out, along with a degree of compromising of each.

Other factors of being compatible are also taken into consideration, and this is where things become intricate, as we will eventually find out it is not a simple walk in the park. If that was not enough, then consider dealing with the intellectual, emotional, physical, and spiritual compatibilities while valuing your self-worth to your mate. Like fitting a jig-saw puzzle, we try to make sense of each piece and determine if it fits appropriately in the overall picture of our relationship.

This situation then presents itself in either soundness of mind or absurdity. I would love to think that neither gender is above the other regardless of how we view each, but unfortunately, this does not negate the fact that we do see things from our own experiences and perspective. These experiences and points of view are expressed in this book and give a behind-the-scenes peek into "him and her" thoughts and actions.

This book mostly focuses on "her" from "his" perspective, but it also spotlights him and creates a setting by addressing various issues in an encounter or relationship while balancing the flaws and merits. Some of these issues are expressed and done in a way to engage the reader while providing several viewpoints. They are purposely done in an animated style to enlighten each subject matter and awaken the reader's subconsciousness while providing a voice to unspoken thoughts. Whether you are a young adult, a middle-aged, or an elderly person, this book will give you an insight into things that are seen through different perspectives and can be applicable in some context. The first chapters deal with conflicts and misunderstandings, then followed by external factors that may affect a relationship, and finally ends with chapters highlighting commitments. The contents of this book are not merely based on him against her, or her against him in a relationship, but deals with the complex issues that has them trying to come to a mutual understanding. The overall intent was not to sugar coat any of the issues but to present them as circumstances that some readers may or may not experience in a relationship. Unrelatable issues do not nullify the fact that they do exist, hence the expression "Raw and Unapologetic."

The stories contained within, are a combination of partially true-life events, and though the book version may generally differ, the overall sentiments remain the same. This book does not act as a cookie-cutter one fits all scenario but does give a consensus. Readers may find some of the contents relatable but should **never** casually link those experience to their own lives, nor should they use it as confirmation on any given subject, though that may be easier said than done. Discretion is advised.

Now that I have gotten that out the way, I invite you to relax and read.

Chapter 1

Can't Live with, Can't Live Without

A small table ornament smashed against the wall missing his head by an inch. Other missiles came flying from her direction as he ducked and weaved his way in the hallway. They had lived together for two years and shared a townhome, but now someone had to go! Whatever the reasons, it became clear that something drastically went wrong. Whatever was quietly simmering below calm waters has now bubbled to the surface. What started as a monotone disagreement has now escalated to a shouting match with flying projectiles. He tries to reason with the aid of hand gestures, but she wasn't having any of that. Eventually, curse words are being exchanged and what was a peaceful happy love nest has become a battleground for staying rights. Broken furniture here and torn garments there. A scuffle and a few scratches are included. The room now looking like an epicenter of a category four hurricane. "Someone, please dial 911!" The drama is now loud enough to spill over into the streets, causing a group of nosey bystanders to gather. The cops finally arrived and as predicted; Ray Charles, "Hit the Road Jack" can be heard playing in everyone's head. It became apparent that he wasn't going to win this battle as he puts his belongings in a box.

He didn't want Tyrone in his business, so he instead, anxiously waits for an Uber cab to pick him up.

Fast-forward six months, and he is sitting by the seaside in his beach attire, sporting dark shades, planting his toes firmly in the sand, and sipping on a piña colada. He is gazing out at the reflection of the sky on a fresh blue ocean with the horizon that never seems to end, running from side to side. A gentle breeze caresses his face, and the only sound present is that of the ocean's splashing waves. To his left is a small carrying case containing a bottle of sunscreen lotion and pair of goggles. And to his right? Yes! To his right is the woman who kicked him to the curb a few months ago, decked out in skimpy red swimwear, comfortably lying belly down on her beach towel with her eyes closed.

It is a perfect example of one of the many rollercoaster epics being displayed and represents the tip of the iceberg, as many others are played out either in public or behind closed doors. The "him and her" represents all of us in some way, shape, or form. Though some of us may not have any noticeable drama in our lives, nevertheless our interaction with the opposite sex can be equally relatable on a smaller scale. The constant interaction of men and women creates enough of these stories to fill virtual space. The major issues for some men are women, and the major issues for some women are men plus whatever sensitive issues they may find worthwhile to argue about. Women! Can't live with them, can't live without them. It is a love-hate relationship on a carousel. This situation not only applies to casual daters or a husband-and-wife relationship; it also applies to any interaction of the opposite sex where a balance of codependence exists. Although you may not have any sort of relationship with that person, someone else does.

The basics of our existence stem from the instinctive attraction of one to another in the continuation of life. Women! Said to be the finer gender. Some are finer than others, but in all due respect, they are appreciated by men, regardless of the situation. They naturally represent our grandmothers, mothers, sisters, nieces, cousins, best friends, fiancées, wives, and depending on your fortunate or unfortunate situation, our exes, regardless of gender. Our introduction to this world is the effort of both sexes, but strangely enough, it does appear that Mother's Day stands a significant recognition to our existence than Father's Day, which many may agree seems like an afterthought. Perhaps it is because she bears the brunt of childbirth by patiently carrying a fetus inside of her until it is mature enough to be separated from her wombs—a truly blessed routine we are all a part of to enter this world. Perhaps it is because she is seen simply as the chief nurturer who is willing to put her life on hold at some point and time for the sake of our arrival. Whatever our reasons, we can conclude that she is looked upon with a general sense of appreciation. Every woman is not a mother but does carry that special motherly instinct to naturally be one, therefore becoming a part of the sorority.

With the spotlight on mothers and women in general, a father will be exposed in a lesser light and is seen as a donor. His title is downplayed to a biological term. You will most likely never hear expressions like "Father Earth," "Father of all wars," or even curse words such as "Father you-know-what." It is also customary to give a feminine name to a sea vessel to ward off misfortunes at sea. Tattoo parlors are filled with hardcore men and boys engraving, "Mom," or a significant woman's name or image, on their body parts.

The comparison between being a mother, a wife, a sibling, or simply a girlfriend may share some similarities but obviously will present each relationship to him on different levels. Her role as a caring mother to a child may not be the same role experienced by some men who became victims of her wrath. He may respect his mother and even love his daughter, but he could show disrespect to his woman. He chooses to argue, fight, and break up with her yet seeks comfort in the same sorority of women. Women act as an unbroken circle in the realm of enticing men, and it is exceptionally rare to see this circle broken. On those few occasions that it does, you will find gay men ironically paying homage to women by displaying feminisms while acknowledging their mothers for their existence through procreation. The creation of Adam and Eve serves as a universal guideline of this natural process of companionship. However, I cannot escape the thought of Adam indulging in a fruit at Eve's request to avoid a hostile confrontation. The expression "Happy wife, happy life" has now become a reality for most men, who must submit to their wives for the sake of peace. If not, then they may have to bear the consequences of a similar fate in the first paragraph of this book.

Chapter 2

Her Wants and Needs?

Some men may ask, "Is this a trick question for women?" While most women will give the same generic answers by not being specific, some men will try to twist themselves into a pretzel to superficially fit the bill. Both men and women can be confused about wants and needs. This has caused some men to be confused as to how to spotlight themselves in the presence of a woman. Women often confuse their wants with basic needs. Wants are her ultimate desire whereas needs serve to fulfill a reasonable purpose. They can be entwined with a sense of balance, but oftentimes walking this tight rope can throw both men and women off track. Young adults who have not quite figured out the reality of life tend to be victims of the wants and needs practice. She may want a shiny red sports car, but what she needs is good transportation. The good transportation could still be a shiny red sports car, but at least her priorities are in place. She may get a sports car then realized it doesn't have an engine. In this case, her choice wasn't practical. She may want a good-looking, wealthy man, but what she needs is a good man. This good man may very well be wealthy and handsome, but at least he fulfills her basic needs. Some women cannot admit their true desires for fear of being judged as being shallow, while some women are unconcerned about what perception others may have of them.

Image is everything, and whether one wants to admit it or not, it takes a special person to hook up with someone who is not easy on the eyes. Being repulsive is quietly swept under the rug and will most likely stay there. If she is attracted to someone who scores no more than a three out of ten on the image charts, then she is utterly unique in her perspective. She tends to be on a deeper level—so deep that some of us would not dare dig but would calmly pass the shovel to someone else with the hopes of them going deep enough to appreciate. Therefore, let's be realistic that a physically decent-looking man is normally first on her list because this is the front page of her relationship, and the importance of a physically pleasing image means a lot to her. Now, before I venture any further, I must explain that it is a natural human trait to be attracted to an image. If not, then the use of cosmetics or any sort of physical enhancement would be unjust. We are all naturally attracted to finer-looking things. This does not mean that it ends there as many spouses who finally settle for their average-looking mates would not exchange them for the world. Image is everything until it is overridden by other factors and qualities. Some women believe that a good-looking man will also enhance their appearance. Of course, women will not admit that it is a prime priority, but who would? She would admit that she is not into how good-looking guys are until she is caught admiring a chiseled face hunk with bedroom eyes, broad shoulders, and thin waistline, often in the company of her significant other. If she is lucky enough, she will eventually get that chiseled face all-around good-looking man she so desires and hope that his other qualities are in shape. Chances are she would be running in denial for as long as possible until the truth that he is missing other essential qualities set her free. Furthermore, there are not many drop-dead gorgeous men or women around to fulfill this fantasy, so this becomes an unrealistic goal for many who may look for some other compatibility to offset physical features. The realistic outcome would be settling with someone far less attractive than what she envisions with his other attributes as a compliment. She will often find out that physical attraction is only skin deep, while his inner quality sucks.

It may also be appropriate for her to say that he must be affectionate, have a great personality, or be on the same compatible levels as her. But to be honest; who would not want these ideal qualities? I have yet to find someone who does not want the same compatibilities, and even stranger yet, they cannot seem to find each other. Though these qualities may vary from one person to the next; may also prove that what they may be looking for in others is what they often lack.

Unfortunately for some, what comes out of the mouth is not what the heart wants. The phrase "A good man is hard to find" may simply mean "A hard man is good to find." Occasionally their true desire may force them to verbally express that he must be great in bed or must be drop-dead gorgeous or rich, but seldom will you hear these words uttered. The reality of him being handsome and a stallion in bed, along with taking care of all her financial obligations for the rest of her life, will conveniently toss the other qualities in the waste bin or allow them to sit on the back burner. Though these factors may be ideal for some women who would like to have a handsome wealthy man who is sexually charged, it does not equal a meaningful relationship on a greater personal level. Couples in a happy relationship tend to sustain it by being spiritually and intellectually connected.

Women are naturally attracted to financially stable men, and in some case play an important part in a decision and is allowed to compensate for his appearance. Though she may also realize that money is not a means to every end, it nevertheless puts her in a secure state of acquiring things for her comfort and securing a family for the future. The two-sided view of an independent woman is to have him bring something substantial to the union or to find a man missing some of the essentials and try to frame him into her ideology of perfection. She may shop for him, dress him up, and even pay for his gym membership so he can become the man she envisions in her dreams. This will work for some until she tries to sculpt him on the inside to her liking, only to find out that a leopard cannot change its spots. Yet for others, it is as simple as finding the right man to secure her financial future or her immediate gratification. The latter may also skillfully play him for what he is currently worth, by keeping him at arm's length until her rightful ship comes floating ashore. Many women may fall under the attraction of the visual spell. These visual spells are exposed in the form of fancy and expensive cars, which oftentimes only serve as bait for the right young gold-digging prey. In most cases, there is nothing much for him to offer other than the passenger seat in his car. Material possessions are normally used as bait to some women who see them as a measure of his success.

A high-profile, good-paying job is closely next on the list as this coincides with "well to do," and is tied to being financially secure. The thought of going out with the garbage collector, a stock room clerk, a lowly paid security guard, or a handyman may not paint a perfect image. Her friends and family may secretly disapprove of his status. His other qualities may need to override the fact that his occupation is not what she had hoped for, and she may compromise if it's worth it. However, once reality sets in and he proves his self-worth, only then will she see him in a favorable light. It is said that the security of a person's future is defined by their state of mind rather than defined by their career. Being a doctor, lawyer, professional athlete, or entertainer does not guarantee financial success. Most wealthy Americans did not necessarily accomplish wealth by a generic occupation or being famous but by their mindset and approach to money.

If she is a younger woman and has a sweet tooth for older men, then she may opt for a sugar daddy, in which case she would become a love interest to a financially established man who in some cases is old enough to be her father and has the funds to venture into this deal. Oftentimes this package deal is wrapped up in sex and lavish gifts to a woman who sees herself of great value in this tradeoff. In cases like these, the sugar daddy will eventually be looking for a replacement once his desires are fulfilled or until she is aware of another candy bar on the sidelines with better options than him, and then he is out of luck. If she is a young attractive devious woman who has met an extremely wealthy widower in his final golden years, and he has a failing heart condition, then it is fair game for her, and she will make sure he puts a ring on her finger and lives out his final moments with a smile on his face. His children and grandchildren may see her as abusing a vulnerable situation or simply taking advantage of their dad, but for him, it's all worth it. He would prefer to live out his fantasy in his final days than die leaving his fortune to a bunch of undeserving family members.

If she is an older woman typically known as a cougar, who is primarily attracted to much younger men, then this will do wonders for her self-esteem. It reveals her confidence to compete for younger men and more so when she gets one. Money is not her immediate concern, but she may choose to cast a blind eye to his obvious faults of being immature, and though this younger guy may not have much to offer her in material wealth, it's mostly the physical attraction of youth and the sexual gratification that has her bending forward to accept someone approximately twenty years younger. The obvious risk in this union would be his constant straying eyes for younger women, who may eventually exceed the perks she offers.

A man who can make her laugh is also complementary; this is a sure-fire way of getting her attention because it makes her feel relaxed and eases tensions in a relationship. Unfortunately, most men ignore this approach when wanting to break the ice and progress to another level. The thought of trying to be a comedian may come off the wrong way for some men who lack a natural sense of humor. Some men fear that this tactic, especially if it is not done naturally, may place them in the dreaded friend zone forever—or worse yet, they could be looked upon as a clown. Instead of getting a long lip-locked kiss at the end of his date, they may get only a friendly pat on the head or shoulder. If he is lucky, he may get a hug that feels like a motherly embrace.

If he is relatively young, has more than one child from a former relationship, without a steady career, then that may spell disaster later in the relationship. There may be some baby mama drama lurking in the wings, with him not able to fully concentrate on bringing home the bacon. A man having a child from an earlier relationship might still have some dirty laundry in his closet to clear out. If not, then he has matured to the point of fulfilling his responsibilities. The only dirty laundry would be a nagging ex who he must endure for the sake of his child. A young woman would prefer a clean slate to work from rather than one that has been written on. If she is mature enough to understand his past and accept him then it's all good. If not, then he may have to pretend that he has a clean slate by lying his butt off until the truth reveals itself in an unexpected visit from his baby mama and the kids.

Her conclusion of a perfect companion in a perfect world would be a physically pleasing image to the eyes along with connecting with her spiritually, emotionally, and intellectually. Someone with a financially secure blanket or the intent to be successful. The truth of the matter is there is nothing wrong with wanting these attributes. The reality of life, however, is different than what we see as a perfect setting. It is understood that she may rightfully want a person who is somewhat compatible with her, with his "A" game intact, but the reality is that she ends up compromising on certain things that she feels is more important to her at the very moment. She tries to balance her wants and hopes that they also fulfill her needs.

The shortest, unattractive, pale-skinned man can surprisingly be transformed to being tall, dark, and handsome by the aid of his red Ferrari and his bank account. The fat, sloppy, disgusting dude she once despised can easily be transformed into a cute, chubby teddy bear by acquiring sudden wealth and showing an interest in her. Some compromising will be done for the sake of her convenience now rather than later. The present-day may be great in holding them together as a couple for a while, but the reality of him not being able to stimulate the relationship on any other level in the future will eventually do him out of it in the long or short run.

Men do whatever it takes to attract women, even to the point of ignoring them to get attention. Sometimes this reverse psychology backfires, and the woman he wants to attract finds love in other places where she is getting her much-needed attention. Some women do not want an easy catch, but at the same time, they do not want to run a mile for that special someone. Oftentimes his actions will be centered around a woman's appeal. We are all in the sales and marketing industry, and whether we admit it or not, we are always trying to portray the best image of ourselves. Our image is our display window, and our actions tell others what's beyond the window. For single men and women, it all boils down to what is in the window display. Men and women are equally enticed by vision, but men tend to get caught up in the image longer than women and don't pay much attention beyond the image until later.

There was a guy a few years ago who would walk around flashing cash while sporting his rich uncle's Lamborghini on weekends to make an impression on the ladies. He would also shop for the latest expensive clothing and return them after wearing them once on dates. Last I heard of him, the ladies caught on to his game. They made sure he spent every dime, and each date was an expensive venture. He eventually got evicted from his rented apartment, his old Toyota was repossessed, and bill collectors were chasing after him.

To sport an image of pretending to be rich or any other attribute to attract another person can put you in a distressing situation in the long or short run. The "Fake it until you make it" is relatable to some people but there is always a hidden price to pay if you didn't make it. People who constantly need validation are prime candidates of insecurity.

A man may think he knows a woman's deep desires—until he finds out he is totally off the charts. What a woman wants can be in the form of a mystery to be solved, and complex as it may appear from one's perspective, it can also be as simple as needing basic companionship. Once she can fully align her wants and needs, then she will be better able to prioritize her desires. For him, there is not much he can do by resorting to his bag of tricks.

Chapter 3

What She Got

A woman will wish for all she wants in a man until she finds out that God purposely did not make any to her exact liking. Yes! He might be the perfect man for her in all his visible qualities. He goes shopping with her, dresses fashionably, has good hygiene, cooks for her, and surprises her with gifts—until she finally finds out that he is not sexually attracted to women and is secretly gay. She may complain that he is too short, too young, too old, or even too nice. It is often said that God has a sense of humor. Be careful what you wish for, or better yet, be specific. I liken it to a lottery drawing out of six. She will not get all six numbers but might get four out of six, or even three. In some rare cases, she may hit the jackpot but simply does not have a clue how to handle the surprise. Some women may say, a lottery is much different as it involves gambling with money, but in all fairness, gambling with your life and time is worse. For women to be satisfied and win their lottery, they must know their priorities. They might not get all, but at least they know which three or four are most important to them. They say you never know what you are looking for until you get what you do not want.

So, she finally ends up with a man who fits the description in her fairy-tale novel: tall, dark, and handsome with an athletic built. He has a good job and makes good money. But then she realizes it's not all it's cracked up to be. He does not spend much time with her and seems to be present only when the thirst of indulging in her cherry is convenient. He traps her by laying his pipe like a skilled plumber at work, and he gives her an allowance to buy her temporary happiness. There is a strong possibility he is also getting his groove somewhere else and keeps her in his trunk as a spare. He is constantly having his ego fed by other women who find him or his possessions attractive and do not find it important or necessary for him to work on any of his inner qualities. Maybe he was attracted to the fleshly image that she originally displayed the night they met and saw her for his pleasures. A long-term commitment was her intent, but his sexual thirst must be quenched before he decides. He may not see her as a wifey material, at least not yet. For now, his ego is out of control, plus he would prefer to see how the chips eventually fall before making a steady commitment.

The vulnerability of some women thinking that their love can be purchased at a price has caused many to become great actresses under this make-believe setting. The reality of men purchasing a brand-new shiny synthetic love would come to the reality that it needs to be waxed over again to maintain that shiny image; if not, one may finally need to make a new purchase to satisfy one's desires. This sometimes leads to a woman becoming a psychological slave in a relationship as the man now becomes a master to her. Affection is not bought—it is earned. She may find the lavish gifts from him a surprise today until the same action is no longer a surprise tomorrow. Now, do not get it twisted, because there is nothing wrong with spending extravagantly on a woman. The point is that most of the time, once the gifts become extremely expensive, lavish, and frequent, the man runs the risk of buying false affection. For the women who fall under these spells, their hearts, minds, and bodies are out of sync. When a woman is truly in love with a man, there is nothing much he can do to convince her any further. Friends and family may try to persuade her that he is not the right man. Finding out that he is not the right companion for her will likely reveal itself on her terms. In contrast, when a man tries to buy a woman's affection, he will eventually find out that someone else will most likely get her for a bargain price much less than he is putting out—or worse yet for him, without any financial output.

A woman's choice out of a selection of men will be determined by her moral compass and standards. This is often reflective of her upbringing and family values. However, social media and friends being an influence over the family will have her ditching her modest upbringing to settle for someone not in sync with her morals and values. If he is cute enough but is a bad influence on her, he will be deserving of her attention; if not, then he will be placed in the bin. Some women with a wider range of acceptance may cast their nets, but often, these women do not see themselves as A-listers or the alphas of the crop; rather, they are down-to-earth and genuine who commonly turns out to be the best and most valuable companions for men whom the A-listers wish they could bag.

For some females, it is all about where he is in life and not so much about where he plans on going. Nothing is exciting about a deprived guy who ironically has a game plan for success in the future, so let us not entertain the thought of knowing him any further. The attraction is simply not there. It is worse if he has the personality of a wall. He is simply looked upon as a nice guy who deserves a pat on the head and a kiss on the cheek, and hopefully, someday, he might find the right woman—bearing in mind it is not her. Mr. Not Happening will be last on the dating circuit unless he has something else up his sleeve like a skilled magician to impress the ladies. On the contrary, some women are fooled into superficial presence until they discover further in the relationship that he is ambitionless and broke.

Women are attracted to strong-willed men, which ironically creates obscurity for what is defined as "weak" and "strong." A man's strength is determined by his boldness and confidence. It can also be determined by his willingness to accept defeat or be apologetic. Unfortunately, some women may see the latter as weakness. Therefore, being too nice is sometimes seen as such. Nice guys are at the bottom of the list for some women because this translates to softness. A guy who never argues or puts up a challenge and is always trying to avoid being on her bad side is an unattractive weakness to some women, and though this can be rightfully defined as such, it is also the exact moment she will pass him off for another mate. The obvious problem then becomes an obscure meaning of the word *"weak"* in relation to *"strong."* With this being the case, some women end up with men who, for them, are a challenge. This challenge unfortunately comes in the form of verbal and physical abuse, yet they see this as strength. The man who finds himself in this scenario will exploit his boldness and confidence to his benefit and ego. She feels that he can protect her from everything, but the reality is that he cannot protect her from himself.

The very few women who feel comfortable in a relationship with a man whom they view as weak tend to have a psychological edge to their advantage, and they use it in a domineering fashion. However, these women must realize that kindness and gentleness should not be confused with weakness.

A woman may also be attracted to a guy as a friend, but for the wrong reason to the guy. She gives the impression that she is interested until after a while he realizes he has become her emotional tampon.

This scenario is when a guy is attracted to a woman, but because of some hidden reasons' unknown to him, she drops him into the friend zone. She does not think of him as a potential sexual partner but rather a shoulder to cry on. The truth of the matter is that most men do not want to end up in the friend zone if their initial intention was to be intimate. Men would prefer to quickly exit instead of being her footstool between her relationships. Some guys do not mind being in the friend zone, and for the woman, it is a refreshing outlet for her, especially if she knows he is already in a committed relationship. But for some single men who fall into this predicament, the women may see them more like a feminine counterpart rather than masculine.

The examples mentioned are mostly exemplified by younger women, but at the end of the day, as she matures, her outlook may begin to change. She may now seek someone who shares her vision and mission, and although these may take on different shapes and forms, the core mission never changes and endures over time. People will go through adjustments in their lives, and whether it is emotional, physical, or intellectual, it will change over time. She may now be better able to identify qualities that are important to her, and in some cases, Mr. Overweight, Mr. Too Nice, Mr. Not Too Confrontational, and Mr. Not Hot may eventually become her choices. She is now winning her lottery. The truth of the matter is that life and time do not stand still, and regardless of how some young women may think now; there is going to come a time when certain standards are dropped.

Chapter 4

"Makes No Sense"

The world we live in is far from perfect, so it should not be surprising that there will be things that do not make sense. This is not necessarily a bad thing unless we spend our whole lives trying to justify everything in our day-to-day experiences. Have you wondered why we unwarily drive on a parkway and park in a driveway? Why are boxing rings square? Why are gifts referred to as free? Isn't all gifts free? When was the last time you paid for a gift? Everything in life does not have to make sense. Some may say that it does not have to be absurd to be classed as nonsense, but to the observer, it surely defies their logic. Trying to make sense of something that does not make sense will leave you in an awkward position of reverting to what was previously said: Trying to make sense of something that does not. I am sure many of you reading this believe you are smarter than someone who is not deserving of the position they are in. Ever wonder why some men never ask for directions even though they are lost? Or why some women advise on relationships, yet their actions are contrary to their beliefs.

Both men and women are perplexing, but some men may argue that irrationality seems to run deeper in women. As I mentioned earlier, this is not necessarily a worst-case scenario, but the poor soul who is trying to make sense of every single issue is faced with the daunting task of figuring out a maze that leads to nowhere. We may see ourselves as the third party looking in at a couple or being the second person trying to understand our partner.

Meet Dante, a guy who dated a young woman in her mid-twenties. She had recently branched out on her own and leased a small studio apartment. She worked as a receptionist at a local law firm in the evenings while juggling her attendance at college to further her education. He got a call from her one morning, and she asked if he could assist her with some cash to purchase gas to commute to work that evening. He then asked her if it was okay to meet him by the gas station close to her home so he could fill up her tank. She said, "Sure, sounds like a plan."

Upon reaching the gas station and recognizing her car, he pulled over and told her to pull up to pump number seven while he went inside and made the purchase. She then hesitated and said that she did not like taking fuel from that station but knew of a better gas station a quarter mile down the street. He then asked her if she had enough gas to get to the other station. She replied, "Yes." He said, "Okay, let's go".

She then hesitated and said, "I thought you were going to give me the money to purchase the gasoline." At this point, he wondered what difference it made whether she purchased it by cash, or he paid with his credit card. Her car tank would be filled in any case. He suspected that she may have had other intentions in mind but could not come up with any logical explanation. If she wanted to borrow money, then she could have easily asked for a loan. This was apparently before Cash App and Zelle, where he could have easily dropped it into her account. It made no sense. I will conclude by not bothering to figure out whether she may be guessing that asking for a loan was a bit too forward or embarrassing instead of asking for assistance for car fuel. Interestingly, they had already known each other for over seven months and been out on several dates. We are left guessing maybe she wanted to physically pay and pump her own fuel. Not being forward on her intention leaves assumptions flying everywhere.

Dante had another awkward encounter with a woman who accompanied him on a date. At this point, we may be thinking he is a magnet for the unexplained. He had hooked up with an intelligent young woman who seemed to have all her priorities in place. They spoke and texted for about five weeks before they finally went on their first date. The venue was his friend's house party. The first thing he noticed upon picking her up from her home was that she seemed a bit insecure about her outfit. This was after he spent an extra hour patiently sitting and waiting on her sofa while she got ready. She wore a cute sky-blue tube dress that appeared too short and tight. It complimented her figure but kept revealing a little too much cleavage while being a bit short. She kept pulling it down because it would reveal much of her lower section but kept pulling it up to hide her cleavage. For the entire evening, she had a tug-of-war with her attire as she kept pulling the top of her dress to cover her tits while simultaneously tugging down her dress toward her knees. It became obvious that there was not enough cloth on this cute little blue dress to go up nor down. Was this a wardrobe malfunction?

He wondered why she agreed to be picked up at 7 p.m. then tells him to wait on her couch until 8 p.m., only to be readily dressed uncomfortably at 9 p.m. It is a mystery for men to see a woman in a public display of adjusting a short dress or a skirt when she suddenly becomes self-aware of her attire. It so happens that the confidence displayed while getting dressed suddenly turns to insecurity upon display in public. If she is going to wear it, then do so with confidence. There is no sense in wandering out into the ocean if you cannot swim. One can only wonder what her initial mindset was when getting dressed.

It is an appreciated sight for most men to see a woman dressed and be in touch with her feminine image, but it is also another thing when that image becomes uncomfortable for her once she is out in public.

Though some men may find her actions asinine, it also doesn't justify his stupidity of driving around with a woman visiting his locale from out of town until it becomes apparent, they are both lost like a blind goose in a snowstorm. He refuses to ask for directions and refuses to use his GPS navigator, as his ego to avoid embarrassment is made known in the form of a knowledgeable tour guide. His eagerness to make sense of his directions for over an hour of driving has his car eventually slowly rolling to a stop as he now realizes his gas tank is empty.

As you can see, men are not too far behind in this "Makes no Sense" issue. He may go as far as complain that she wears too much makeup on her face, while he publicly wears his trousers below his butt cheeks.

Some other notable examples of her that may have him scratching his head include surprising her with a new car, lavish jewelry, taking her on exclusive vacation getaways, and fancy diners only to discover that it's the smaller details that make her happy, or she complains to her friends how cheap he is, for giving her only a rose or a small necklace while trying to stay within his limited budget on any expenses. If he does not display any emotions or cry on the outside, he may be looked upon as insensitive; if he shows emotion and sheds a tear or two, he may be looked upon as being weak. If he has a collection of women to choose from to go on a date, he may be looked upon as a player. If he has none and cannot find a woman to go on a shopping spree, he may be looked upon as a loser. She may tell him to go hang out with his boys and then get upset with him when he does. She may say, "Be honest and tell me the truth. I promise I won't be upset." Then when he does, she gets upset. In this case, her request for an answer is a dare and not a request. She emphatically hates being lied to but would freely be dishonest to save herself if the situation presented itself. She does not call him, because she is too busy with work, school, kids, or whatever excuse it takes to prevent a two-minute call or text. If he does not call her within the same period, then those same excuses are not valid. She admires the closeness he shares with his mother but complains he is a momma's boy. She wants him to be bold but sees him as being too forward. If he is assertive towards her, he is too aggressive, if he is unobtrusive then he may be gay.

Onlookers may find it surprising when the woman they had great expectations; ends up tying the knot with a loud, self-centered, abusive jerk, and she always finds an excuse to defend his behavior. Much abuse has been dished out in the name of love and reveals itself in the form of swollen cheeks, eyes, and welts on her skin. Lies have been told to cover up this insane torture of love: "I bumped into a door." "I fell and hit my face on the pavement." The few who do tell the truth may have you wishing they had kept silent or may have you feeling good that they are confiding in someone. "We were just having a little squabble over a minor issue. We both will be okay." Some may even complain that a man should take charge, but when it comes to making the important decisions, her first and last words seal the deal. The list of honorable mentions includes being offended by derogatory terms yet singing along to derogatory songs. She complains about "Where are all the good men?" and then goes to a club or bar and expecting to find them there. She dresses in revealing outfits and then complains that he wants her only for her body.

Books have been written on the secrets of understanding a woman. These so-called self-help books of knowledge have aided some men in more ways to better their relationships. However, it does not prove the man who may now claim he is an expert when that cute, charming, cheerful woman he dates turns out to be a psycho.

This story about George and Cindy serves as an example in this setting. George met Cindy through a mutual friend and was convinced this was the woman for him. He was a good-looking, career-oriented guy, and she was a physical fitness trainer. They eventually went on their first date, and all went well as they got to know each other's likes and dislikes. Cindy was a trophy catch in Mike's eyesight. She was witty and charming with flowing long hair and bright green eyes. She was a perfect ten, and every physical feature seemed to be in the right proportion. She was the type of woman whom almost every young man (and probably an old man) would have loved to have on his arm. He was no doubt the envy of his friends. After dating for six months, they decided to move in together.

A year into the relationship, he noticed that she had become increasingly demanding of his attention and would question his whereabouts like a detective fishing for information. She would call him or text him at least twenty times per day and expected an immediate response each time. When they were together in public, he could not look at any other woman, and many times he would be falsely accused of having wandering eyes. George had no idea why she would have been like this and did not have anything to hide; he was not cheating on her. She would nevertheless search through his possessions when he was asleep or away, and she would demand access to his phone log. It went to the extreme where she bought a tracker for his car to monitor his every move, and she even showed up unannounced at his office's after-work social gathering, which was an awkward situation for him.

It became apparent as time progressed that every single moment for George became a living hell. He eventually told her he needed some space to rethink the relationship. It all came crashing down abruptly a few weeks later when she silently stood behind him and eavesdropped on the last portion of his phone conversation. The last words he said before being clobbered over the head and left temporarily unconscious were, "Love you too." We must be wondering what his mother was thinking after closing the conversation by saying, "Love you, son," and then heard a screaming woman on the other end cursing her out before hanging up. The only thing I can say about this is that sometimes the candy is not as sweet as it looks. Cindy's action does not make any sense even to the most discerning woman. The respect we have for people, along with the way we perceive them, sometimes does not exactly pan out for us to make sense of it.

The following setup may have some people asking, "Why?" This one involves both genders, and it may not be a bad idea for some, but all hell breaks loose when this situation predictably plays out.

The digital clock on the side table had just changed to 2:30 p.m., and the sun's rays entered the room at an angle. The ceiling fan was at a moderate speed to relieve the heat of that hot summer day. The only sounds that could be heard within the four walls of this setting, was the shrieking sounds of an old mattress with worn-out springs and the heavy panting and gasping of air accompanied with groans as Avery and Zak indulged their bodies in the ecstasy of the moment like a grinding mill at a factory warehouse. They lost all awareness of time in their immediate surroundings of dusty furniture, scattered shoes, and clothing. If that was all they lost awareness of; then the story of two consenting adults doing the deed is none of our business, but the cell phone video she agreed to have him strategically place on the windowsill to capture this event, bought us all in as willing or unwilling spectators.

With selfies and video recording becoming increasingly popular and overriding common sense, they decided for whatever reasons to capture this event to replay over as potential porn stars in their movie. This was only between them, but unfortunately, a recording may unintentionally bring this X-rated showdown into the mainstream of family, friends, and even enemies. The trust that is instilled in another human to not share may be a movie premiere to a wider audience. For her, the image she originally portrayed in the minds of family, friends, and enemies may be overridden by this new release, and all perception of her was changed. Whether it was for the better or worse, depends on who was asked. For him, the fellas may realize that he lied to them by not truly admitting to oral sex.

The quest for capturing an image continues as two lovebirds decided to take a selfie together on a small stone ledge hanging over a cliff. The ledge could barely accommodate both. Yes, you guessed correctly. It did break and they fell below. Luckily, their fall was only fifteen feet into a river. They both survived without injury. The phone was lost.

The next short example also serves as a third party looking in on a situation. This also has to do with lust and secret desires, but when it is a middle-aged pastor of a small church and his wife, then it has been elevated to the "makes no sense" category. Both were at a venue where they were not expected to see each other. Let's just say that whether he found her to be more intriguing is totally up to him. I am sure she did not expect him to be a customer, nor did he expected her to be the entertainer. Sometimes an outward image does not match inner desires. But who are we to point a finger as the next "Makes no Sense" examples might be our actions.

Chapter 5

She Detests Him

Some of these women are carrying stacks of luggage. Yes! They are the very ones who have been ripped to shreds in rough relationships. They have been wounded so badly that it has left an everlasting scar on their hearts that cannot be hidden. They walk around with heavy baggage from their past, and their hearts are damaged and seem irreparable. This damage develops into hate. If it is not her, then more than likely it is her girlfriend, or someone close who has given up on men by giving them the middle finger.

This vicious hate sometimes starts as early as childhood. They hate their fathers for not being there for their mothers. In some cases, they may not have a clue who he is, hoping he and their ex-boyfriend rot in hell. They would be happy to supply Satan with some wood and it would be an honor for them to ignite the flames and watch them burn. This unfortunate circumstance is coupled with a bunch of failed relationships, one after the other. The last one was the most brutal as dishonesty, infidelity, and ass-whupping played a vital role in the saga.

She has tried to make the relationship work, sacrificing her body along with some blood, sweat, and tears, but to no avail. She sees all men—not some, but all men—as four-legged creatures. She does not want to have anything to do with them in any way, shape, or form unless it is totally benefiting her.

It is sad to say that many women fall into this category, but it becomes even sadder when the only child they have is a boy. Two things can then happen. She can unleash her anger and retribution on the innocent child, causing him to grow up with anger issues and be abusive to women in the future, or, unaware to her, this very child would be nurtured in her loving care only to meet a woman in the future who shares her thought process, seeking revenge—and her son is the victim. If she has a daughter, then naturally she will instill this fear and hatred of men unto her child.

To hate all men could play like a vicious circle of hate and in time could lead right back to whoever dishes it out. Once the hating stops, the healing starts. Instead of running to a girlfriend who shares her passion of hate for men, she finds a friend who has a good relationship with her mate or a couple that has been happily married. In the initial stages, this might make her feel even more unfortunate as envy may swirl in her mind, but in time it will make her feel better. In some ill-fated cases, her rejection of him leads to a sexual bond with her now newfound female companion who just happens to have the same opinion about men. This sometimes turns into an emotional attraction for each other, more like something that was not planned but due to circumstances fell right in their laps. Females now readily and freely admit without any remorse that they are lesbians. The so-called excuse of "being curious" tends to justify their actions. One thing is for sure: you will never hear a guy say, "To hell with women. I think I am going to be gay from now on." A heterosexual male will never choose this as an alternative. He will keep threading the waters until he strikes gold.

This next story I am about to share is based on my personal experience many years ago. Meet Britney, an attractive young woman in her late twenties who apparently has been through rough times in her past relationships. I met her as a co-worker at a call center, and whether it was her fault or her unfortunate choices of men in her life, I truly could not tell and I did not really care at that moment because of her physical attraction, more than anything else, pulled me in. Her repellant demeanor toward men seemed like a worthwhile challenge, and I saw her as a diamond in the rough, waiting to be appreciated. I was somewhat successful in engaging her in a conversation. I told her that all men are not alike and that someday she might find the right guy. As the days turn into weeks, I continually tried to persuade her to go out on a date but would hear a bit of hostility in her rejection. "Been there, done that, and heard that before," was her reply. The only success I had was her taking my number, but I quickly realized she may have taken the number out of sympathy and ditched it, while I was making futile attempts to have at least one date with her. I then began to question my motives in what seemed to be an impossible task. I decided to throw in the towel, call it quits, and move on.

About a month later, out of the blue, my phone rang. It was her. She had called me up wanting to go out. I found it strange and shocking that she had my number despite the fact I gave it to her. I figured she must have felt sympathetic toward me and decided to do me a favor, but that thought was quickly erased when I foolishly believed she may have tried to conceal her attraction toward me. Whatever the reasons, I felt chosen by the holy one to finally give men a good name. She had mentioned that she liked to take long walks on the beach at night, so I mentioned the beach as an option after having dinner at a popular seafood diner. Her reply was, "Sometimes it's too lonely, dark, and quiet on the beach, and I do not trust any man. I have a fear of being raped." She immediately bought me back to her reality and perspective of men, and I silently questioned her motive for calling me up for this date.

I got her address and picked her up, and we went to an American diner on the strip. At the diner, she kept staring at a guy and his woman a few tables to my left. She then said, "I bet those two over there are cheating on their mates."

I asked her, "How did you come to that conclusion?"

She replied, "They both came in separate cars, and I could have sworn I saw him with a different woman somewhere." She paused for a few seconds and then added, "Men are like dogs."

I responded in her favor by distancing myself. "Yeah, some of them can be like dogs." I tried to sway the conversation to a less toxic topic, but by then she was looking at her phone and laughing at some text messages she had received. She then decided to show me a photo on her phone of an unmarked grave and said she uses that picture to psychologically bury her past relationships. This creeped me out and scared the hell out of me. I now thought that it was the burial site of all her ex-boyfriends, but somehow, I could not get past the thought of such a cute girl doing such an act.

The server finally came over and presented us with our meals. She kept covering her mouth while she ate, but I figured it was simply a part of a strange evening. After dinner, I offered to take care of the bill. Her reply was, "I will pay for myself. I don't want any man to think that I owe him anything after dinner." I then realized that she wanted to vent her pent-up feelings, so I did not feel offended by her response.

The night dragged on, and she decided she wanted to go to a casual club not too far away. Upon reaching the club, which was within walking distance, she boldly paid her own admission and bought her own drink. It was not long after that I began to question my purpose on this date. I figured that she must need someone to dance with. Yes, we did dance to reggae and hip-hop by standing approximately seven feet apart, but as soon as a slow jam would start, she would noticeably hurry back to her seat. Strangely enough, she would be content with moving her shoulders and hips to the beat of the music while swaying her head slowly.

This long nightmare of a date that seemed to come from the abyss of a red fiery furnace, was finally winding down to an end. The club was slowly clearing out, and we sat and drank casually. I was glad it was coming to an end while I pretended to listen to her babbling about Charles, an ex-boyfriend that I reminded her of. A couple of minutes later, I could not help but tune her out, I could see her lips moving but couldn't tell what she was saying, and strangely enough, I could hear "The Star-Spangled Banner" being played in my head as I blankly stared into her eyes. Only God knew what Charles did to her or what she ultimately did to Charles. My only silent thoughts were that wherever Charles was at that very moment, he must be happier than I was—and most likely he was relieved that she was out of his life.

I was relieved the date was over but regretted I had gone through with it. There was an awkward silence as we drove back to her place, and I came to terms and reasoned with myself that I was more of a therapeutic outlet for her. I gently pulled up my car to her driveway after what seemed to be the longest car ride over the shortest distance. I was in the process of sarcastically telling her it was an interesting evening, but before the car came to a complete stop, she opened the door and jumped out. I asked her, what's the rush. She then replied, "No kisses on this date." I was shocked that she thought I would have done such an act. It was not like we had a romantic evening together. I tried to be courteous by not driving off until she was safely in her house, but for some strange reason the lower half of my torso was not cooperative, and my right foot seemed to have other plans as it hit the gas pedal and I barely saw her go through the front door of her home.

She continued working at the call center for a few more days until she vanished, and I never saw her again. The only advice I can give in this scenario is that if any man happens to come across a woman like Britney, please, run fast in the opposite direction.

Chapter 6

She Can Do without Him

Can she do without him? Some women, after gaining a fair amount of success in life; give the impression that they do not need a man. They have somehow overcome or conquered the thought of a significant other by replacing it with their own spotlight and glory. They walk around with their heads high and stand on a podium only a perfectionist could possibly reach. She looks at the average man with scorn as she conceals herself by rolling up the tinted windows of her shiny new Red Mercedes-Benz and apply her makeup while driving. More than likely, her initial thought of a companion is someone who she can happily do without financially. She will insistently state that she does not need a man to support her. She now looks at most men below her status not as social companions but as inconveniences. If approached, she may immediately think he is chasing the goods between her legs or her pocketbook. Under no circumstances is she going to submit herself to anything that is not going to bolster her profile. She may even desire to have a child, but the father acts only as a sperm donor.

Chances are, some of these women were soiled in a bad relationship, and they now think men want their money, or they do not want men because of their past experiences. She may have found him cheating on her after she has invested her emotions, time and money in the relationship, leaves her struggling with their child or he may have been financially supporting her until it abruptly stopped for another woman. He may have torn her heart out and trampled on it. Whatever the experience; it certainly was not pleasant. She is now in a better position to cancel him and other men from her life. Her financial status has changed for the better and her standards are now so high that it cancels out ninety nine percent of men.

These are the same women who secretly invest in adult toys to satisfy the hidden thirst they get at night as they toss and turn in their king-size beds. The dildo with two triple-A batteries has now become the faithful, trusted sexual partner, ready to go at the flip of a switch. They are the very ones who would secretly share with their girlfriends what brand sex toys gives the best stimulation. They discretely look at the bulging trousers of men without anyone noticing. This whole charade has to do with too much false pride in women. The make-belief that a man is not needed is exactly what it is: make-belief.

Then gradually, she comes to terms with the fact that she cannot be okay in the long run. A basic human need is to have someone in her corner when times get rough. The girlfriends she so faithfully holds on to might stab her in the back simply for her having more than they do. She may be going through some emotional crisis and need the reassuring voice of a man, letting her know that things will be okay. She could be laid up in the hospital and away from family members. In some cases, she may need a home or appliance repair, and the companion of a good handyman around the house would save her tons of money that she would have spent on a problem that sometimes does not even exist. She will temporarily make friends with a gay guy to superficially fill the void until she finds out his femininity falls short of her natural yearning for a real man.

In contrast, men often do not give special attention to these women, especially those of high status. Some men may even think they are lesbians due to their actions. The truth of the matter is that whether she is a high-earning executive at a major company or flipping burgers at a local joint, she will still be looked upon as been equal in his vision. A man's head is where he is getting that good loving. Ever wonder why some men cheat on their mates while all appears to be perfection on the surface? An executive for a major corporation may very well lose her boyfriend or even her husband to the housekeeper. Guys are not attracted to the possessions of a woman but see her as an attractive member of the opposite sex; the other attributes are of secondary importance.

The very few who manage to involve themselves in a relationship will no doubt now wear the trousers in the union. They will not allow the man to be a man. They genuinely believe they know it all, can do it all, and have it all. This creates a toxic relationship because the man now seems insignificant in his role. Worse yet, she may have a little celebrity status or managerial position at work, and then she brings that same diva attitude or bossy mentality to the relationship at home, acting like she is still in her professional surroundings. She does not know how to be strong without being dominating. Some women do not know how to balance themselves, and that is why we have immensely powerful, successful women being single, or the man is simply keeping quiet while trading off the benefits of the relationship. She may be in a better position now than when she was being taken advantage of by her ex-boyfriend; but should in no way try to replace a natural union of companionship with too much pride.

The false pride displayed in the idea that "I can do fine on my own and do not need a man" has to do with too much self-confidence, to the destruction of communal thoughts. There is absolutely nothing wrong with having everything and being independent. It is only wrong when some women use it as a valid excuse to seclude themselves from men. Using anything other than the desire to have a God-given human companion to fill a void is a void that is not filled.

Chapter 7

The Age and Weight Scale

Age and weight are the two issues some women refuse to discuss under any circumstance. Most men think that discussing it is a forbidden act in the Bible. The bathroom scale and the scale of time exist only as a constant reminder of our imperfection. The thought of being in your twenties with a slim youthful appearance tends to linger in the mind rather than physically as the golden years approach. The constant purchasing of weight-loss supplements, seasonal gym visits, plastic surgery, and liposuction have made the quest for perfection a billion-dollar industry in a country that, ironically, has the unhealthiest foods available at any given moment.

Cosmetics, plastic surgery, supplements, and health gurus have women trying to maintain their appearance or turn back time. Though the intention of being the best you can be is understood, oftentimes it leads to an unreachable, unsatisfying goal. Whether it is done for self-improvement or due to a lack of self-confidence could reveal itself as good or bad. I have never heard a woman say she is totally satisfied with her body. Swimwear and lingerie models are not satisfied with their physique, and you will find the skinniest woman complaining that she is too fat. This seems to bother women more than men and eventually becomes an insecurity issue. The quest for perfection would let it seems like there is a curse on the body. Gaining weight is a natural reaction of our bodies to dieting, lifestyle, and metabolism. Wrinkles and sagging skin are our body's reactions to time. Metabolism however does also play an integral part as we get older, therefore, adding a little more weight in our later years. Though the thought of losing weight and maintaining a youthful appearance is appreciated; it must not outweigh the appreciation for life and self-worth.

Meet Rosetta, twenty-six years old. She is in extremely good shape and works out to stay fit. She works for an advertising firm, and often a sales deal is made on the mere decision of her appearance, which has her on the frontline of the company as their spokesperson. Her job is extremely competitive because it calls for younger, vibrant women in her position who may be better able to convince others that they are making a fantastic choice to do the advertisement for their respective companies. This area of competing is like any other example and can be dangerous for women who often lose control of themselves to hold on to time. Now, bear in mind that she was twenty-six when she started working for her company. She also met and got married to Patrick, and the union lasted for eight years until she got a divorce. She was single for two years until she met Scott, and they had a relationship for four years. If you were doing the math, she refuses to admit that she is now forty and a little overweight. She unwillingly trains younger sales associates to do what she started out doing.

For the women who age gracefully, it is all about the state of mind and not the body. Aging is simply God's way of telling us it is not all about us; it is about what we do and whom we affect. Very rarely will you find a loving couple complaining about their age or weight. Oversized women are normally last on the list for most men, which in turn puts great pressure on trying to be slim to catch a potential mate. A woman should never lose weight to please a man because she will still be disappointed at the end of the day trying to live up to someone's expectations of her.

The modeling industry, along with the constant portrayal of youthfulness, has revolutionized the world's outlook and ironically causes many to go to the extreme of malnutrition or anorexia to acquire a youthful appearance. The main thing she should remember is not to get caught up in the frenzy of the industries that are out to get rich from her discomfort. She may have bought a dozen weight-loss supplements, and her gym membership dips in her checking account every month whether she uses it or not. She may have made the same New Year's resolution every year. It does not make her feel any better until she feels good about herself on the inside. The thought of losing weight to fit into that swimwear for summer or any other special occasion is good. However, it is living a healthy lifestyle that makes her comfortable—that is what counts in the long run. There is absolutely nothing wrong with taking care of herself and trying to maintain a youthful image, but often the latter falls short of her expectations and leads to depression. Being content is having peace of mind in knowing that she is healthy, unique, and special to that lucky man. The sorority of full-figured women who see themselves as curvaceous goddesses is constantly on the rise. And finally, it is much better to age gracefully with the expectation of adding some weight than to die young while looking like a model. The choice is hers. Whether women choose to hide their age and weight is totally up to them. One thing I know for sure is that being twenty-six for five years straight and holding on to a slender figure may seem okay, but after ten years, she should let it go.

This next story is about Pamela, twenty-nine years old, cute, chubby, and adorable with a bubbly personality. Ingrid was her best friend, and they would sometimes hang out together on weekends. Ingrid had a steady boyfriend, Fred, whom she had met on a blind date two years earlier that was recommended by another close friend, and obviously, it turned out well. Pamela did not have that special guy in her life and hoped that someday she may meet that lucky man to sweep her off her feet. This is where Kory comes into the picture.

It was at about 10:00 a.m. and the breakfast café was relatively busy. Pamela was sipping on a hot cup of coffee and nonchalantly browsing through her phone while waiting for Ingrid and her boyfriend to join her. A text message then popped up. "We are running a little late. Traffic backup. Be there in about ten minutes." Pamela replied, "Take your time. I already reserved seating." She then temporarily glanced up from her phone and noticed a guy seated across the room staring at her. Without hesitation, she looked down at her phone and continued browsing. She would occasionally look up to see if he was still staring. Yes, he was! She clumsily looked away and presumed it was a coincidence that their eyes met.

As she was busily engaged in her browsing, she was interrupted by a voice. "Having breakfast alone, or waiting on someone?" She glanced up to see the same guy standing at her table. He had a cute smile, was well-groomed, and wore a cologne with an inherently masculine, invigorating scent. Before she could respond, he continued. "Hi, my name is Kory."

From what she saw in his approach and confidence, she replied, "I am Pamela. Most people just call me Pam." She hesitated for a second. "I am waiting on my girlfriend and her fiancé to have breakfast. They should be here shortly."

He said, "That's fine, but I would love the chance for us to have breakfast together next time. I was waiting on my bill when I saw you sitting by yourself." She blushed, they then quickly exchanged numbers. Then simultaneously, Ingrid and her boyfriend entered and passed him on his way out.

They texted and called each other for about two weeks before they saw each other on their first date. In that time, she got to knew him and learned that he was dealing with the sudden passing of his grandfather. She was consoling as he opened his feelings to her. Pamela knew this could turn into something meaningful as she senses a bit of closeness between them. The yearly summer art fair was in town, so they decided to go after realizing they both loved the arts. He picked her up in his car and drove to the venue. The initial reception was fine, but as the evening progressed, Kory became increasingly distanced from her. She did not think much about it and chalked it up to his grief over the loss of his grandfather, whom he was remarkably close with. Nevertheless, she enjoyed the afternoon out with him and looked forward to him warming up to her next time. The dated ended with an innocent embrace after he accompanied her to her door.

She shared her experience with Ingrid, who was happy for her and gave her words of encouragement. But as time progressed, the phone calls and texting from Kory became noticeably less. On one of the few occasions that they spoke, Kory had mentioned that his birthday was approaching. Pamela used this opportunity to initiate a second date if he had nothing planned on his birthday. They eventually decided to go on his birthday to dine at Scrumptious, a popular spot where it was also customary for a live band to be present.

The day arrived, and she called him early and greeted him with birthday wishes. They then confirmed for later at 6:30 p.m., but he told her he would meet her there instead of picking her up. It was no problem for her because she had her transportation, and the only inconvenience would be parking in the downtown area. She wore a nice burgundy dress that she had recently bought and had her hair done for the occasion. She also bought him a small gift wrapped in a box and a birthday card.

She arrived at the appointed time but noticed he was not there yet. She secured seating for two and ordered a drink while she waited. She told the waitress that it was her companion's birthday because it was customary for the staff to present a small slice of cake with a candle to the recipient, along with singing the popular birthday song.

It was now 6:50 p.m., and she was getting a bit anxious when she got a text on her phone. "Be there soon."

She responded, "Okay, I am here. See you when you get here." Her anxiety went away, and she felt a bit at ease knowing that he would be there soon. She started browsing through her phone and in no time realized that it was now 7:30 p.m. She called him, but the phone went to voicemail after several rings. She texted, "I am still waiting. Are you close by?" Still yet no response. She was now on her third drink, and occasionally the staff members would glance over at her to see if he had arrived.

It was 7:45 p.m., and it was obvious something was drastically wrong. At 7:50, a text from him finally popped up. "I don't know how to say this, but you are not my type."

She quickly responded, "What do you mean, I am not your type?"

He replied, "You are overweight, and I am not attracted to obesity."

She quickly responded with tears filling her eyes, "Didn't you notice that when we first met?"

A few minutes passed, and then she got a response. "I met you when you were sitting down and had no clue that you were that big, and the clothing you had on did not reveal much. I didn't want to hurt you but decided to let you know. I am sorry, but that's all I have to say. Bye."

Tears flowed down her cheeks as she nervously took a napkin from her bag and wiped away the tears. One of the staff members, sensing that something was wrong, came over to console her. Pamela calmly stuffed the card and small gift into her pocketbook and sat there for five minutes to gather herself while the band coincidentally played a song that reflected the mood. A male staffer covered her expense and gave her a fifty-dollar gift certificate from the restaurant. Her heart was broken. She felt like being in a dark sunken space. Not being appreciated for who she was, felt like salt poured in an open wound. She wanted to disappear and put this behind her as much as possible. She would stare at herself in the mirror and blamed herself for how she looked. As the days went by, her self-confidence lessened and occasionally a tear would roll down her cheeks. Her notable cheerful persona was visibly absent.

This unfortunate incident shows the reality of rejection for some women, and many of us cannot utterly understand its' pain under such circumstances. However, the story doesn't end there for Pamela. She decided to join a gym with her best friend Ingrid who acted as a source of inspiration. With the aid of a personal trainer and a nutritionist, they both made slight adjustments to their diets. This was done naturally to feel better about themselves rather than to please someone's perceptions.

Fast-forward seven months later, and Pamela is transformed into a slimmer version of her former self. Her self-confidence grew over that period, and she was back to being her cheerful self. She now dates Gregory, a much better-looking guy than the one who had formerly rejected her, but the real bonus was revealed when one day she jokingly asked him, "If I gain some weight, would you still be with me?" His response without hesitation was, "There would be more for me to love." Her outward response was a smile, but the real joy was internally felt in her heart. She did gain a few pounds in the months after, but Gregory sealed his promise with an engagement ring. The rest is history.

Chapter 8

Greener Grass on the Other Side

It is a known fact that women want men that are desired by other women. They are competitive by nature. This catch-22 plays out uniquely as she finally wins him over without realizing that the attraction of other women doesn't end on her watch. This does not only apply to unmarried couples but married couples as well. The same basic reasons for her attraction to him as a single man desired by other women is the same basic attraction for her and other women once he is committed to marriage.

Single women fantasizing over a married man and the ability to snatch him away from his love nest is one of those strange wonders that ironically isn't strange at all. A woman must realize that it's not every woman shares her values of respect. The fear of a mistress lurking outside of their happy home can be a traumatizing experience. It is a known fact that some single women tend to daydream over men who are already taken. It somehow seems attractive because he is committed to a relationship. Things sometimes seem better when viewed from across the river. It is somewhat a challenge for her to take what is not hers. It is sometimes a fulfilling feeling for a woman to be a mistress and likewise for the man to have one. She may have programmed herself to believe she is more satisfying than his girlfriend or wife, which somehow gives her the feeling that she can fill whatever void is there to be filled. With her uncontrolled emotions being an obvious factor, she will be staring at a reflection of herself in his current mate's position if places were switched.

This has caused some men to freely admit they are married or casually dating, knowing that they are attracting women rather than rejecting them. In some cases, he is damned if he does and damned if he does not. Some men will certainly succumb to the temptation of a woman eager to steal or borrow him, especially if his relationship becomes dull and the love fades. The attraction stems from both a lack of stability and a sense of commitment. Being married gives the impression of stability and commitment, but strangely and ironically, it opens the doors to other women who find this appealing for their own personal reasons.

Women who fall under the spell of married men, or men who fall under the enchantment of a married woman, are most likely not trusting of each other once they finally get together. If he decides to hang out with the boys after work, it might cause a problem for her. He may also show some insecurity about her whereabouts. In cases like these, the grass is always greener on the other side until you cross over only to find out it is artificial turf. You rarely find a man willingly venturing into the realm of a married woman unless he is enticed by the woman to cross that threshold. If her husband found out about her infidelity may not only be detrimental to her but also to the intruder.

The story I am about to tell you is about Judy and Simon. They met on a website. This was not your normal dating website but more a social outlet for introducing, corresponding and making new friends—which of course could be used for the very same reason as a dating site. Simon had noted in his profile that he was married, and Judy's profile stated that she was single, so naturally, she was aware of the situation that he was already taken. However, his cute, charming smile and description of his likes left an open invitation for Judy, who presumed he must be unhappy to be making friends with another woman on the Internet. Judy was also an attractive woman with distinguished cheekbones and bright eyes. Simon's profile was up for about two weeks with the right words and description, and it attracted the right fish at the right time. They got to know each other by examining their profiles.

They began corresponding and eventually exchanged cell phone numbers. A month later, they then started to date. She told him that she shared an apartment with a nosey cousin who kept preying into her business, so therefore they would meet discreetly at a Starbucks. This went on for about two months and became a regular practice. Starbucks became their regular pickup and drop-off location. They would sometimes sit in his car and kiss for a good five minutes before finally saying goodbye.

On one occasion, a Wednesday, he asked her to spend the weekend with him at his timeshare home on the beach. She replied, "Sounds great. I will let you know by Friday." Friday came, and she agreed. They then met at a central location, and both went in her car.

The property was approximately two hours away in a picturesque, wooded forest filled with tall oak trees that cascaded down to a view of a stone-filled beach and bright blue ocean. His cottage was one of many that were built distance from each other for privacy reasons. Aside from a drizzle upon arriving, the weather was perfect that weekend as they freely indulged in each other's company. They cooked, hiked, and did water sports. The evenings would be capped off with a glass of wine while watching the sunset. They continued to see each other discretely as the weeks went by.

A few weeks later, on a Sunday afternoon, Simon and his wife, Natalia, were on their way to the mall. A police trooper on a bike pulled up beside them and signaled him to stop. Simon quickly glanced down at his speedometer to make sure he was not going above the speed limit, and he confirmed he was doing forty in a forty-five zone. The police went over to the driver's window and signaled him to open his window. As soon as the window was down, the trooper asked, "Do you have any idea why you have been stopped?" Simon replied, "No". The trooper went into a small leather case he had strapped over his left shoulders and presented a picture of Judy. He asked Simon, "Do you know this lady?" Simon now realized it was not a traffic stop, but with a puzzled look on his face, he said "No." The trooper lowered his shades and peeked over them as he got a clearer glance at Simon's wife. He said, "Ma'am, do you know this lady?" Obviously being more confused than Simon, she shrugged her shoulders with a discerning look on her face and replied, "No."

The trooper then pulled out a cluster of pictures from his bike compartment. These pictures had Simon and Judy together. He showed Simon the pictures and said, "These were taken last week. Do you have any recollection of her now?"

Simon awkwardly replied, "Ah, yes, I now remember. She was a friend who was having some problems, and I gave her some advice." By this time, Natalia was suspicious of foul play.

The trooper then asked, "Do you normally do comfort therapy a whole weekend at your place on the beach?"

Simon's wife was now breathing fire, and she too wanted an explanation. He had told her that he had spent the weekend camping and fishing with business partners.

Simon then asked, "Is she okay? Did something happen to her?"

The trooper calmly fixed his shades on his face and placed the pictures back in his bike compartment. He got back on his bike and said, "She is okay. Just wanted to meet the person cheating with my fiancée." He then rode off in the opposite direction.

Obviously, Simon and Judy decided to drink from the fountain of disloyalty rather than faithfulness. Simon eventually got a divorce and the trooper ditched Judy. Judy and Simon are now officially together but are both watching each other like hawks. No word on the trooper and Natalia. I will keep you posted.

Chapter 9

She Got Stabbed in the Back

Women seem to do things as companions that a man will dare not do with his friends. I can never recall a man saying, "Hey, Gary, wait for me. I am going to the restroom with you." Though this may be an innocent act, it's not normal for a heterosexual male to do. Some men are even uncomfortable using a urinal next to another man.

It seems that the camaraderie women have with one another is unrivaled by any other species on earth. The constant sharing of personal effects along with a needed shoulder to cry on has fooled many naïve women in the realm of this friendly setting. There is nothing more fulfilling than this display of girlfriend closeness, and often it is hard to tell whether this closeness goes beyond just friends. But under this façade of deception is the reality that females will betray each other. Whatever intimate moment she revealed is used against her. Like Judas running wild with a blade in an open crowd, many backs will be slashed. The power of slashing is done when her back is turned. She will be gossiped about. Her grandmother may have warned her that "Your ears will start to ring when someone is gossiping about you." If she believes it hasn't happened to her yet, then she is naïve to the sins of gossip.

Women will gossip as friends among each other, and then as soon as the group splits, they will gossip again in a smaller group about the friends they just left. There is a high chance if Jacky and Marilyn are gossiping about Abigail; then Abigail and Marylin are also gossiping about Jacky. There is absolutely no one above this gossip mill and escaping it may mean one simply does not have any "frenemy." They would talk, laugh, eat, and drink with her and then as soon as her back is turned, betrayal, lies and hurtful gossip takes over. The wounds of backstabbing burn even more, when she realizes it was someone she confided in and trusted.

In the corporate workforce, it becomes more obvious because the gossip mill is constantly churning out juicy stories of misfortune along with the constant competing and elbowing to get recognition while climbing the ladder of success. This whole action spreads faster than any cold during flu season. Guys will let females know what their objective is, or women can sense it, but women will smile with girlfriends and say, "Hey girlfriend, what's up?" They really mean to say, "Bitch, where is the money you owe me?"

The obvious use of the word "backstabbers" is self-explanatory, and females will never see it coming. Backstabbing has become so popular in mainstream media that most reality shows are based on that concept. Producers are making tons of money off unforeseen dramas and the reactions of the victims and viewers. It is for these reasons that some females prefer to keep males as closer friends because it is harder to detect a genuine female friend from one with a six-inch knife waiting to slash her in the back at the right moment. Whenever a man becomes great friends with a woman without any strings attached, it always turns out to be a better relationship than with a woman. Some women are natural-born stabbers. Women who walk around with inflicted wounds by the hands of their formerly trusted girlfriends will understand this situation better than most.

Chapter 10

Kids or No Kids

Kids or no kids? That is the question. The blessing of having a child is exactly what it is. But some couples may want to press the pause button and hold off on the idea of having a child until the relationship matures past a certain level. This is much easier said than done, as raging hormones are more in control than anything else. The spontaneous joy of not having to attend to a crying child who craves attention every second is something that can be appreciated by all in its perspective. The freedom and joy of walking butt naked around the house, getting busy wherever you choose and making as much noise as possible are some of the many trade-offs of not having a child too soon. Romantic trips and weekend getaways can be planned in a flash without shipping the child to his or her grandparents. If a relationship is not strong enough or mature enough to accompany a child in the mix, then it will likely fall apart inch by inch as both partners lose out on the quality time needed to spend together without the perplexing issues of a third party. This sometimes also extends to single men and women weighing the consequences of their future potential mates, and although there can be some advantages to having them early, it's always a sacrifice for him and her.

Men will occasionally check the backseats of women's cars to see if there is a baby seat. If one is present, that may spell a few different scenarios for him and her. The first impression it gives is that she has a boyfriend or is married, and the child is the by-product of a settled relationship. The second impression it gives is that she does not have a boyfriend and does not care for one at present due to her undivided attention to her young offspring, coupled with the lack of support or the absence of a father. The third impression is that she would love to have a man provide some comfort for her, which indirectly would also help her child. Some guys may see this as an opportunity to get her hooked, and they see the child simply as an extension of her and do not mind the trade-off. Hey! I am just being real about different scenarios. A woman must also realize that she cannot control the thoughts of other people, so in no way should this bother her if she has a child seat in her car.

It can be totally unfair for a woman or man with a child to be looked upon as not being accepted in the dating scene for fear of a crazy past relationship or the dividing of attention. It is also hard for a woman once she finds a boyfriend because she must now wisely juggle her time between her new mate and having a babysitter. A mother who may be spending more time with her baby than a father who fled the nest may send a confusing signal to her new mate, who may feel like he is jostling for attention. Not many men can balance a relationship with a single woman who has a child. This situation presents itself like walking on eggshells, and sometimes the woman does not make it easier on the guy, who now must become a friend to the child while not acting like a dad. I recalled an incident where the guy had to include five-year-old daughter on his dates. The two obvious things that may happen, are, he may break under the pressure, or she may find him extremely patient and tolerant to her situation.

On many occasions, a woman lets it be known that her child is the world to her. Some women may find this admirable if a single father expresses the same sentiment for his child in a dwindling group of men. On many occasions, a woman will let it be known that her child is the world to her. Some women may find this admirable if a single father expresses the same sentiment for his child in a dwindling group of men. In rare cases, she may prefer him not having kids, but, in most cases, her motherly instinct would take over. If they are in a relationship and had children from a prior relationship, then she may prioritize hers over his. The act of looking at the kids as an additional burden on their relationship may temporarily weigh on their conscience until a family bond is created.

Some men, due to their careless play, irresponsible acts, and lack of communication with their baby mothers have been caught in the dilemma of paying child support, often to a woman who sees this as an excellent way of getting revenge. The child support money may go toward her getting a manicure, pedicure, and regular visits to the hairdresser. In some cases, this money that is sometimes automatically subtracted from his paycheck after Uncle Sam takes his fair share, is spent on supporting another man in her life. But who are we to cast a judgment? There are no words etched in stone regarding how a woman should spend this child support money providing the child's care and needs are met.

At the end of the day, kids are a blessing and should be looked upon as such, not as a burden. The problem is when the blessing becomes a curse for single mothers who keep having kids with the same man in a failing relationship. There seems to be no logical explanation for such action, and it can only be surmised that she is a woman who obviously not only cannot control her thirst for sex but also has an uncontrollable appetite to have kids under the same failing conditions. Shame on her! Notice I did not blame the father. I doubt the father placed a gun to her head and ordered her clothes off, face down and ass up … or maybe he did! We hope not.

He may, however, not realize he is creating his downfall, and her girlfriends can never figure out her situation and summed it up to being under his spell. It does appear, however, that there may be some hidden trade-offs in these dilemmas. Depending on her mindset, she may see the kids as tax benefits, and the more kids, the bigger the payout.

Many women may feel that the desire to have a child or two is a mandatory thing. It is truly a blessing to have a child refer to her as mommy as she takes on motherhood before the clock stops ticking. But to think that it is necessary to be a mother, though beautiful as it may seem, is wrong. "Be fruitful and multiply," must be taken in context. If there is no suitable partner to have a child with, then so be it. God is fully aware of the fact that it takes two to tango under ideal circumstances.

Following closely in this ordeal are the deadbeat dads who ignore their kids. You may see a few of them in a club or a bar nearby you, looking for their next victim. They seem to be very notorious and need no introduction. Almost every single mother will tell you about them. If not, then ask the kids the last time they saw their dad. The few who show up now and then, as an occasional doctor's visit in their children's lives, have their children doing the daunting task of trying to find a suitable and truthful Father's Day card with appropriate words to fit.

If a man frequently mentions his child in a conversation, then there is a good chance he is taking care of that child. We never seem to hear about those faithful fathers who stand by their kids and support them all the way, and whether the mother is a part of this support system or not seems to be totally irrelevant. Then there are the faithful men who take on the brave task of fathering children that are not biologically theirs. These brave soldiers are as scarce as gold. You will hear about women who became parents of kids who are not theirs, but you do not hear of the man who took on a woman with six kids and shouldered the responsibility of raising them.

Last but surely not least are the men who would love to give support to their kids but cannot seem to find the child's mother, who apparently is in a good financial position to hide and shield the confused child. That child may now think that the father has abandoned them. Though this occurrence may be rare, it does exist. The Internet has helped in tracking her, but to get any sort of cooperation is another story. We never seem to hear about these rare mothers who use their children as some sort of revenge or payback to fathers who would love to support their kids. Chances are, they blend in with mothers who have good-for-nothing baby fathers and disguise themselves as single mothers. It is sad to say that some mothers consciously use their child as payback for a dispute or some drama that occurred years ago. This bitter feeling of hate runs deep, and forgiveness or reconciliation is never an option for them. Reconciling should be sought for the sake of the child, no matter what the circumstances were. The bottom line is that the child is always entitled to know his or her biological father, whether he is serving a life sentence in prison or due to some drama that was played out with the mother years ago.

If a man needs to see his kid or wants to share custody, provided it is passed by the courts, then let it be. Not spending time with or not knowing your biological parents is like an empty space that regrettably cannot be filled, especially in cases where the biological parent is deceased. There is no explanation that can justify this act of self-gratification by a woman to the detriment of a child. A mother who uses her child for revenge or lies about the father is never a good thing. Likewise, a man who does not support his child or is not a part of their lives is just as bad. There should always be a middle ground of reconciling to benefit the child. Having a child is an added blessing, not an added curse—though some kids would have you swearing that they came from hell to torment you for the rest of your life and serve as a constant reminder of how quickly we age. Nevertheless, it is the sharing of that intimate, explosive moment that he and she once experienced that results in children present in their lives.

Chapter 11

Reading the Signs

A woman will frequently think she has her man figured out, especially if they have been together for a lengthy period. She will also try to create a profile of a man in less than fifteen minutes after an initial introduction. Oftentimes these misconceptions are so off the charts that they belong to a different area code altogether. Briefly, his actions may seem like bad news, but if read properly they can prove meaningful to the relationship and save time. The opposite is also true. A guy who is interested in his woman and has factored her into his future will show signs. Likewise, if he does not, it will be apparent.

If a guy has a bone to pick with his woman or challenges her in a debate, it should not always be looked upon as a negative or him being on the warpath to end the relationship. If he is questioning her whereabouts, workaholic hours, or spending habits, or he simply did not like a situation involving them, it may mean he cares enough to venture into the forbidden without the thought of suffering the consequences. The big plus is that he is comfortable with the relationship without worrying that a little friction may cause a permanent problem. This may be easier said than done for some men, as the big minus would then be him being kicked to the curb for being too argumentative. He may end up sleeping on the couch for a whole week. But the point made here is that wise men rarely choose to argue with a woman, so when he does it may be for a good reason. At least, we hope.

If they recently started to date and he gets angry for the simplest reasons, along with being assertive and constantly confesses his love for her then by all means he is a psycho. If he speaks with his eyes more than he does with his mouth along with no fluidity on subject matters and timing, then he is a creep.

The other great misconception contrary to the one last mention is silence. The golden silence of being quiet without saying a word while sharing each other's company is something that most couples cannot deeply appreciate. A woman may be thinking if he is quiet, then something is wrong with him. That may be true for women, who are like still waters that run deep. There may be anger boiling over in that moment of silence. If her response is, "I am fine, don't worry about it," then this may not be good for him. On the contrary, his silence can be translated to being content and comfortable with the relationship. He does not have to prove that he is not boring by starting a meaningless conversation. A man would generally prefer to listen rather than talk; he would rather be an open ear to her complaints and concerns without uttering a word. Ever try taking a long journey with your significant other who insists on talking up a storm until it gets into a debate, and then you end up arguing and finally having an all-out fight? Many of these long car rides that were supposed to be a pleasant journey on a fun-filled weekend getaway, turned out to be a fight at the steering wheel. Yes! Believe it or not, there was a couple who was arguing back and forth, and it turned into a hostile shouting match. They did not even hear the siren or notice the flashing red lights of a state trooper who was trying to stop them. Nor did they realize that they were going twenty miles per hour above the speed limit. From what I understood, this conversation calmly started out with talking about the weather, and for some strange reason, an hour later it ended up with screaming and arguing over a celebrity whom neither of them personally knew.

Gaps in a conversation may feel a bit awkward at first, but as couples grow to appreciate each other's company, silence becomes golden. Oftentimes both are guilty of talking too much which can reveal some insecurities or simply being misunderstood, causing all hopes of being together flushed down the drain.

A woman may complain that her man does not do the things he used to do when they first met. She may complain that he does not wine and dine her as he would have previously done or taken her to the movies or concerts as often as in the past. She may feel he is slacking in his actions toward her. Though I must admit that it is good to keep the flame burning by doing these things, women must realize that that same flame is burning on a different level. He may want to cook a good home meal and share it with her at his place with candlelight, soft music, and all the settings of a truly romantic evening—or he wishes she could do the same. Going to the movies may be okay but cannot compare with cuddling with each other and making it a movie night. Eating out may be great at first, but in the latter part of the relationship, it does not compare to him or her preparing a good home-cooked meal with candlelight, which is where real intimacy ignites. These actions give a reflection of who he really is, and they give her insight as they both settle into commitment. It is practical for any man to take a woman out on a date in the initial stages, however, in the latter stages, a real companion will reveal something much more important than what the average man would do on a first date. This is where his identity as a person who factored her in his future is revealed.

One can understand that a somewhat perfect atmosphere must present itself in the initial stages. That includes being with the right person, going to the right places, saying the right words, and doing the right deeds. But once this phase has passed, that's where true romance begins. Because of this scenario, you can easily spot couples who have just hooked up and the ones who do not have to show public affection or outward actions to prove themselves worthy of being together.

The type of date will determine not only his or her personality but also the amount and type of interaction. Physical contact can be very natural in some settings but unsuitable in others. Dining out is usually the first option and can be used to get to know the person through conversation. Questions and answers will flow throughout the evening without much interruption. This stage is for those who see it as necessary to talk before easing into second gear.

Men should also realize that there is no guarantee of any show of affection after a date, and the lobster or prime steak dinner will not justify the amount of affection received once the date has ended. However, a showing of appreciation by her would be expected. His appreciation of her is already revealed in asking her out, taking her on the date, and picking up the tab, therefore it becomes a matter of etiquette on her to show some sort of appreciation. Depending on how the date went, or how much she is into him along with her values, can be revealed in the form of a handshake, hug, kiss, or sex.

If a handshake is presented, then the date has turned into a friendly business meeting. The type of hug will determine the level of affection or appreciation. If it feels like a quick motherly hug, then she doesn't want him to feel bad about his efforts. If it's an embrace that lasts for more than 10 seconds, then she is feeling him, with the possibility of a kiss if she is ready. A quick peck on the cheek may signal good intent for a second date but must be combined with other positive body language to determine his or her future fate. A long-locked kiss may be the ideal situation for most men and is only done when she sees him as a potential future date. This is usually done in sync. A one-way locked lip kiss from him may cause a sudden disaster.

Jumping in bed on the first date may be immediately gratifying for both, but he may reconsider her values once he has left her presence.

Attending a concert is also good, but only if the performer is a favorite of both. You can expect to get to know each other during a concert but it is done through the sharing of good times in acknowledging the performance, which may bring great memories for both in the future if all goes well. Touching may seem awkward if the timing is off and especially if a conversation is not flowing.

Clubs, parties, or any other social gathering where music is played may present an opportunity for touching and gentle caressing, and that can often prove whether there is any physical chemistry going on for both partners. In general, dates are geared toward the person's individual likings and can be a good way to become close with potential mates if similar interest is shared.

Shopping can also be a sign of good intent. The honesty of liking a gift and appreciating the effort can be a welcoming action for both. He or she does not have to honestly like the gift to be appreciative. Sometimes it is the effort and sincerity that are more valuable than the gift. Imagine a scenario where she is at a Department Store returning a Christmas gift she bought for her boyfriend. It was a nice expensive watch. She can be heard telling the salesperson that her boyfriend said he would not be caught dead wearing that ugly thing on his wrist. You could tell in her voice that she was hurt by his response, and the salesperson understanding the situation, did not bother picking out another watch for her to purchase. The refund was placed back on her card, and she seemed very satisfied as she made her way to the women's shoe department.

Couples that are more in sync with each other may not have this unfortunate experience. If a man knows what she likes, then that man should be a keeper. Likewise, if a woman knows her boyfriend's taste and style and gets him something that he genuinely would like, then she is a keeper. This simply means they have grown to know each other's taste in style.

We have all seen the men and women who would sacrifice their comfort to please their significant other. Oftentimes the temperature of affection can be determined when both are shopping for a home. If either of them is not compromising anything, then it is a one-sided affair of self-gratification. The man cave he anticipated having turned out to be an additional closet space for her bags and shoes. He does not have to ask which closet or bathroom is his because the size will inevitably determine hers. It is customary for a woman to have a ton of stuff to store, and she may need more space because her clothing and added accessories are variations and are more sophisticated than his. But the true test may be in the form of her offering to take the smaller closet and bath for his sake and comfort. Hey! I know this is impossible, so this is all hypothetical; but for the one lucky man in the world presented with this offer from his girlfriend, he should immediately put a ring on her finger. When the house is purchased or leased, he should make sure she is comfortable by giving her the larger closet and bathroom along with setting her bubble bath every evening with lit candles and rose petals. He may also occasionally throw in a bottle of her favorite wine while she is soaking in her bathtub. She is a keeper.

Chapter 12

Will She Ever Ask Him Out?

Should a woman ask a man out on a date? There is no law against this practice, and there is no written code that a man should always be the pursuer, though this is the usual trend. If a woman makes the first move, then she is unfairly judged as being too forward. If she sees someone she likes, then she may flirt around and throw out subtle hints with the hopes of him reading the signs and biting at her bait. This may not be the case in most instances, and a woman may miss the chance of making that first move to be with her knight in shining armor.

Women ask for equality with men but seem to be selective on what is equal and what is not. If a woman is good enough to wear trousers, then she is good enough to make the first move. We were brought up by society to believe that the man should be the chaser and the woman should sit and wait, but many times the waiting turns into desperation, frustration, and finally eternity. I would like to believe that the ancient concept of waiting went out with the 1960s generation, along with the Beatles, and Woodstock; if not, then we would be watching a black-and-white television, lining up to use the phone booth in public, and dancing to rock and roll music.

Women are continuously taking the place of men. Yes! What do they call it? Gender equality. It so happens that this "equality" is based on the convenience of cherry pickings. I believe that equality should be expressed in more ways than one. You may blame equality for the death of the stay-at-home mom. They have almost become extinct and are only currently recognized as soccer moms, who, under ideal conditions, would be out there in the workforce. From what I gather, it was a regular trend up to the 1960s, but there was a drastic change in the 1970s, mostly due to single parenting and the emerging need for women to enter the workforce. They now deservingly should get equal pay as men and in some cases more, which should also allow them to take the place of men and take the initiative of asking them out.

Women are now ready to join the military and fight shoulder to shoulder with men on the frontlines, but they are scared as hell to ask men out on dates. Some women would prefer to conveniently partake in everything except the act of asking a man out with the fear of being rejected. If he rejects her offer, she may look at it as an insult, and if he accepts, she may look at it as a risky investment. Oftentimes the women who think of it as a risky investment also prove themselves guilty of being a risky investment for some men who expect a show of affection after a date.

Many times, a good opportunity can pass because women did not take the initiative. Some men may view this as a refreshing change. Guys are constantly asking women out and being rejected for whatever reasons, yet they still walk around and live normal lives. The greatest regret is for her to look back in life and regret the list of things she did not do and what could have happened. It is her life, so she should take charge.

The great irony to this situation is in one's perspective. Picture yourself as the parent of your sweet princess who is rejected by some random guy rather than him working to gain her affection and asking her out. I am sure every father would feel the same about this situation. If there are any words of advice from a parent to a daughter, they are to present subtle hints and hope the guy is smart enough to recognize them.

The other irony of this situation is if she sees herself as a princess within her rights; then she may not want to make the first move under any circumstances. However, beauty is in the eyes of the prince, who she may hope is attracted to her enough to make the first move.

Chapter 13

The Breakup

This one seems to affect everyone at some point and time in their lives. Whether it was a high school sweetheart or a recent loved one, very rarely will you see a breakup end on good terms, and often one person is wishing it did not have to occur. Text messages and phone calls become less frequent, and the words "I love you" cease to exist in a conversation. The awkward silence that now dominates has taken over for the worst and not the better. She may choose to fight over the simplest of things and dig up faults out of nowhere to justify her exit without feeling guilty. He may be straightforward and say, "It's over," if he has someone else lurking in the shadows. She may say, "I need some space to figure out stuff."

Both women and men know the consequences of a breakup and the effect it has on the other. That is the main reason why it is sometimes done subtly under the pretense of needing more space or more time to figure out life. The less they speak, or the less he sees her means the relationship will slowly dissolve into an affair that ceases to exist. Whatever the case, the thoughts of living happily ever after were only thoughts and not a reality. The bodily tattoos of his and her names have tattoo artists creatively disguising these marks.

The true reality of a breakup will reveal itself in the form of a rejected broken heart. Sometimes this event is played out most viciously. Cars have been spray-painted with obscene language, windows have been smashed, and tires have been slashed as grief turns to anger in the spotlight of rejection. The shared good times no longer linger in the thoughts, and photos of happier times and love notes have been deleted or shredded. The innocent teddy bears are either ripped to pieces or cuddled for comfort in this dilemma. Hardcore men and self-centered women succumb to this reality of a broken heart under waterfalls of tears. To know that he was once the love of her life yesterday and is being replaced today will have grown men secretly crying tomorrow once the reality sets in that she is gone. There may have been certain warning signs that eventually triggered this action of departure but were ignored due to the thought of the relationship being unshakable. The reality of this is that it is a dirty job that he or she must do for the sake of moving on.

In other rare cases, the relationship may be emotionally charged, and she displays a wide variety of mood swings in a short duration, therefore taking the relationship on a crazy roller-coaster ride until it comes to a stop, and he gladly steps off in relief, still being slightly disoriented but intact. In this case, both are satisfied, as she finally ends it, and he gladly goes his separate ways.

A breakup or a divorce on good terms, where both parties contently agree it is not worthwhile to be together, often proves someone is waiting in the shadows to take over the relationship. Very rarely do two people depart on satisfactory terms without someone else lurking in the shadows unless both cannot stand the mere sight of each other, which would not be the case if they got together in the first place. The thought of having his or her eyes on someone else, serving as a security blanket, will make this process much easier. The rejected man who got kicked to the curb would land on softer ground if there was a woman somewhere out there to cushion his fall. If not, then the thought of some other man enjoying what was formerly his; will have him stalking his ex-girlfriend day and night. For her, she will have one foot in a shaky relationship while the other foot is seeking firmer ground. Once both legs are planted firmly on solid ground, she will officially end the relationship. She now inhales a breath of fresh air and takes on this new venture with the hopes of not gasping for air in the future. But for now, her true feelings are attached to one guy, and she does not have to hide it anymore. In other cases, for her to end a relationship without getting emotionally attached to another man will reveal that her partner has failed miserably in her expectations, and she would prefer to be lonely rather than share herself.

The impression that a relationship can end on a positive note is oftentimes a misconception. The man who finds himself in the position on the verge of losing the love of his life should never try to win her back by begging and presenting her with flowers. She needs space to reason with herself while he is out of the picture. It is a total turnoff for her to see him in a weak position of craving after her when she has already emotionally checked out. If he is the one to end the relationship, then she will have the emotional support of family and friends to cushion her fall. If she ends the relationship, then he won't have much emotional support from anyone other than his cats and dogs. As they say…he would have to man-up to the situation. For her, the ending of one book is oftentimes the beginning of another filled with excitement and thrills. Her attention to Mr. Reject subsides as her interest in Mr. Accept grows. In cases where she discreetly dumps Mr. Reject and pursues Mr. Accept, it is to make her not feel outwardly guilty of her actions as he weeps over his loss. Any outward display of regret in the presence of him or her should be avoided for the sake of one's dignity. However, closet weeping is recommended for the sake of relieving a heavy heart.

With the advent of social media and texting, breakups are now being done with less personal interaction and with little or no remorse because there was not much of a personal connection in the first place for either to have any true emotions. After having a relationship for a year, she suddenly texts him, "We are done. It's over!" He then replies, "Okay! Did I leave my phone charger in your car?" Some people are more concerned about losing a relationship with their phone than a person.

For most of us, whether male or female, the bottom line is that no one wants to be rejected in a relationship—unless of course, a suitable alternative exists, or a bond was not created over a significant amount of time. Women will opt out of a relationship quicker than men, and although this may seem like a negative mark, it also serves as positive because she values her intimate emotions and sees them as exclusive more than men value theirs. If he is not up to her expectations, then most likely she may be starting another book with a colorful cover and interesting title. Let us hope the contents are good.

Chapter 14

Plain as Black and White

Whether you like chocolate or vanilla, coffee with or without cream, or ebony over ivory, the obvious difference apart from texture and or taste is in shade or color. The shades black and white are at the far opposite ends of the color chart, with multiple shades in between. Unfortunately, it also acts as a racial classifier and skin color specifier. If you are Asian, Indian, or Hispanic and consider yourself not a part of this distinct group; you do share certain traits from colored and white folks. The issues dealt with in this chapter are very relevant to each group but are not immediately noticeable until they present themselves as an obvious problem. I wrote this segment and explained it as clearly as possible, but some people will naturally disagree with some of the points, as with any other topic in this book. To interestingly mix the shades black and white, you will get grey, which is not only another color but unfairly sums up the situation for many interracial relationships.

We tend to agree that a black-and-white relationship can be challenging for both parties. This issue is often swept under the rug and avoided but somehow raises its head at the opportune time. Before we delve into the relationship aspect of this scenario, let us look at the words *prejudice* and *racism*. Racism is the belief that a race or skin color is superior to another, whereas prejudice is a prejudging that lacks reason or experience. Therefore, anyone can be prejudice toward a situation. Racism is caused by hatred, whereas prejudice is out of ignorance. Because racism has more destructive qualities than prejudice, it can be illegal and result in civil or even criminal penalties in some cases, where renting or selling a home or applying for employment can be used to determine the severity of charges in a crime. Due to racism institutionalization within the believer's mindset, it unfortunately can also be used as safe grounds when referring to a relationship being exclusive among a race. It is our prerogatives on choice or preference. Anyway, I know what you are saying, so enough of the explanation—let us get down to the issue of men and women black and white. Regrettably, the explanation plays a vital part in this segment, which perceptibly may not apply to everyone's relationship on black and white. But without probing into the different nuances of ethnic background and geological differences, most will agree that the color barrier that presents itself within racial boundaries can get even more complex when dealing with interracial relationships. The expression "Jungle fever," comes to mind, and I am not referring to a severe form of malaria but rather the attraction of one race to another. It is natural to be attracted to the opposite sex, but when we factor in the word *"interracial,"* then the relationship comes with heavy baggage due to disparity in opinions.

We may see a black man with a white woman after being successful, it's like, "Now that I have attained extreme success, what's missing? Oh, yeah, a white woman. Good—that should teach all of them black women a lesson." It is his way of saying, "See? I am just as acceptable as the white man and need no approval from my race."

Some black women look at this as a slap in the face, and the very few black men who make it to the top, go for someone different from their complexion. The truth of the matter is that some of these same black women are the ones who give black men a hard time. They are also the same women who class black men as worthless bunch of good-for-nothings. Some look at black men like dogs, not to be confused with their cute little pet Chihuahuas. It may seem unfair for a black man to make such a choice after enormous success, but most black guys who would date a white woman over a black woman do so because of the many social issues a black woman puts forward or brings into a relationship. For him, it is a matter of too much red tape. Symbolically speaking, if he puts his car in drive, there is red tape in front of him. If he is in reverse, there is red tape behind him. If he tries to open his car door, there is red tape outside. She may demand a lot of attention but rarely gives. She constantly looks for so much without realizing and appreciating the good she has in her hand. She sees him like a heavy bag of coins worth ten dollars rather than a light bag of bills worth a thousand dollars. She has been told one too many times by her mother and other women that she is a queen—without trying to become one. Many times, her idea of a strong black woman is to stand in opposition to black men. All this, coupled with a list of emotional baggage and petty issues longer than her hair extensions, is the prime reason black men seek a companion in fairer pastures.

A white man who settles for a black princess sees himself as the ultimate warrior in a forest of black men. Though they came from different ethnic backgrounds, he somehow manages to woo her based on intellectual interests. In some cases, she feels more secure because the underlining factor above all may be fiscally in her favor. Shockingly, he may be prejudice against some blacks but is not racist. He sees his black princess as an exotic trophy and does not mind her standing out amongst his friends. He will treat her like a genuine princess and value her input. He sees her as unreplaceable and feels like this chocolate and vanilla union was a match made in heaven. She feels accepted, and it did not take much for him to win her over because more than likely, she has a hidden affection for white men. The trick for him was to find her among other black beauties who may cast a blind eye to him if he appears average. She displays certain qualities that are refreshing to him. She is accepted into his family except for a few mutterings and murmuring from his distant relatives. She feels a sense of stability in the relationship and occasionally compares in her mind to dating Dexter Black. You will never hear of any quarrels or abuse to her, though we are not sure whether they are good at concealing it or just not in his nature or fear of dealing with her crazy relatives.

In contrast, if a white woman decides to go beyond the color barrier and stigma to accept Dexter Black in a relationship, this says a lot about her in a positive light. She is quickly recognized as neither racist nor prejudice and values her black stallion and his race for what it is worth. His opinions are valued over his black counterpart. If he is wealthy, then she has bagged a gem and sees herself as a prime catch. If Dexter is fine-looking, the only cons would be a jealous black woman or a curious white man. Dexter's family may need to warm up to the occasion but will eventually accept her in the family. He now feels accepted across color barriers and not seen as just another black guy who is unappreciated by his peers. If he is not financially established, then the challenges will be a little more difficult for her. Friends and family may be wondering if she bumped her head.

Her parents would be politically correct by emphatically stating, "We are not racist." This expression is posted in their conscience like a lit sign to anybody who cares to know. The inevitable test would be in the form of her dating or being engaged to Dexter. One out of two things will happen. Dexter would be genuinely accepted with open arms as her boyfriend or their new son-in-law, or he would be rejected, and all hell breaks loose for him and his white fiancée. In the latter case, Mr. Black is a fine young gentleman if he stays on his side of the color barrier. The "We are not racist" sign is subtly deactivated. If her family is not financially well-off and Mr. Black is filthy rich, then the "We are not racist" sign will subtly reactivate with some consideration.

A financially secure black woman may never submit herself to a broke white dude, and although this is not impossible, the occurrence of it happening is extremely rare. You may have a higher chance of spotting a whale in the ocean. In her mind, it would not make sense for her to cross the color boundary and submit herself to what she could have easily done without going the extra mile. This is also true of a wealthy white woman who would dare not submit herself to a dark-skinned man who may be constantly strapped for cash. If she is a wealthy white cougar seeking a young black stallion, then clearly, he would be on sale, ready to be purchased.

The issue of interracial couples is overly complex and presents different layers of problems not only internal between them and their immediate families but also externally to friends and strangers. A black woman may not like to see her black girlfriend with a handsome white man. She also may not like to see a fine, dark-skinned man having the time of his life with a white woman. "How dare he be happy and content without anyone who doesn't look like me." Unfortunately, that is the same sentiment carried through by both blacks and whites and reflects as, "How dare the person to be happy in an interracial relationship when my race is not a factor of this happiness." The thought may naturally surface and then quickly disappear once we check ourselves; if not, then it lingers on to the point of thinking, "How could this be possible?" If the thought lingers on and materializes into outward actions, it is reflected as racism.

Frequently a sense of betrayal is seen from the perspective of the observer rather than the interracial couple. A black guy may see a black woman with a white man and feel betrayed, though he would run into the arms of an attractive white woman if the opportunity presents itself. He displays intolerance toward the black woman's choice due to his insecure mindset, which is proven by his final act of running into the arms of a white woman. Though racism is often defined by an outward act, it's mostly our hidden thoughts that truly define us.

The couples in an interracial relationship do not see their actions as a betrayal to their respective races but are focus on the acceptance of each other. Nevertheless, the insecurities that present themselves can be in the form of consequences such as Black Ebony's preference for light-skinned black brothers backfiring when he ignores her for White Ivory. This insecurity may extend further to the point of her hooking up with Tom White for the sole purpose of her child having white features. Women who are guilty of such practices normally see themselves as black curses rather than colored beauties.

The upbringing and social indifferences are marked contrasts for blacks and whites. A black woman may not be as free-spirited as her white counterpart, and her openness to ideas and the natural zest for life may be limited to a certain extent. However, this may not be all negative in some respects because the pressure of high expectations and achieving her goals at hand is foremost rather than allowing her to explore and enjoy the simple pleasures of abundant life. There is a higher possibility that somewhere in her white colleague's family, there is wealth; though it may not be directly connected to her white friend, nevertheless it is in the family pipeline. Black Ebony's combined family worth may be equal to one of White Ivory's relatives living in another state or overseas. With that mental mindset, White Ivory's grasp and appreciation for life are more obvious than Black Ebony's. It is a natural tendency for White Ivory to join a gym, go jogging, go on long trips, take a cruise, attend a concert, visit a recreational park, entwine with nature, have a pet, walk her dog, join a club, or indulge in some creative activity. For Black Ebony, this may not be the case, especially if she is younger than thirty years old. Her range is much smaller and sometimes is limited to her immediate surroundings and comfort level without exploring beyond. Dexter Black is also of no help to her because he too is limited in his knowledge, his actions, and the comfort of his immediate surroundings. Dexter and Ebony can break loose only when they expand their horizon. This horizon is not necessarily in the form of roaming in white pastures but in freeing themselves from the stigmas that have been placed upon their race.

Their vibrant and rich cultural background, along with high expectations in general, unfortunately and ironically, reveals itself in the form of unnecessary bickering that is sometimes subconsciously played out in a black relationship. Dexter and Ebony are at a psychological disadvantage where the under-the-rug issue of race discrimination is concerned. They are then left with some insecurity, causing them to be victims of their selves. Dexter is constantly being watched and judged not only by whites but also by Ebony. She is also watched and judged not only by her peers, who expect a certain standard of her but by White Ivory, who may see her in a lesser light. A group of young white females casually dressed and sitting on the floor at an airport in the waiting area paints a different picture if a group of black girls did the same. A white man helping an elderly black woman may be an accepted sight, but a black man helping an elderly white woman may be a suspect of an attempted robbery. The setting that each portrays is unfairly judged in its appearance. The guilt of this judgment is unfortunately inclusive of both races. For black women and men, the fear of rejection is constantly over their heads, and whether they admit it or not, trickles into other areas and reflects their insecurities. White Ivory dating Dexter Black may immediately signal that White Ivory is not racist, but in Dexter's case, he is seen as a sellout.

As you may have already noticed, an interracial relationship can be as complex as the science of the human body, but it should be defined simply as an affection for others that is indiscriminating of color or race. The restrictions on interracial marriages were outlawed decades ago, but unfortunately, some people still carry the stain of racism by their mere presence. The freedom to choose is our civil right. These civil rights are then filled with our desires and motives. These desires and motives act as mirror images of our hearts. Whether or not you choose to mix your vanilla with chocolate or your coffee with cream, it all boils down to your taste and benefits.

Chapter 15

Her Parents' Blessings or Approval

She is going through with the plans, and her parents did not give their approval. Whether they like it or not, it is going to happen. One can only hope that Grandma and the rest of the family gave her their blessing and well-wishes. She is now an adult but still respects Mummy and Daddy, and hopefully, they respect her choice. My reasoning is partially due to the decisive alternate choices made by some women. A mother, father, and daughter coming to a full agreement on a perfect husband-to-be is as rare as UFO sightings. Someone is silently disapproving of the union. The parents will accept him due to love, respect, and well-wishes, but in most cases, they will think their child deserves better. This has most men falsely believing that the acceptance by parents qualifies them as a perfect candidate for their daughters.

Behind closed doors, this upsets parents when their beloved daughter, whom they sent to college and nurtured in love and care, chooses someone they feel unworthy of their princess. This has caused many parents to silently say words such as, "Out of all the good men out there is this the best she could find, after all the money we spent on her?" "What has become of our daughter?" The doctor or lawyer they were hoping their daughter would finally marry to secure her future, and in some cases, what is left of theirs, turns out to be the art student pursuing an uncertain music career. His show of love and devotion for his girlfriend over the past several years now has approvals and blessings suspended in mid-air. To be or not to be? That is the question. This situation has also caused some women to conveniently hide their boyfriends, knowing that they fell a notch or two on the scale of worthiness in their parents' expectations. This also creates a stressful situation when the marriage knot is tied, and her parents are closely monitoring every step, and things do not run as smoothly as they had expected.

The other scenario is her ex is no longer in the picture, but because of the mother's outward approval of him, he is now in a lasting friendship with the mother. Guys who do this believe that if they win over the mother, they might eventually win over the daughter. Yeah, sure! Keep dreaming. He may choose to give up on her father because he is usually reluctant to greenlight any approval. Her father sees every man as a reflection of what his thought process was at that age. The father barely trusts the man his beloved daughter has chosen to date or, worse yet, get engaged. He can only hope he is a loving and caring boyfriend who is not a sex freak like he was when he met her mom back in his days, that can financially support his little princess and protect her from danger.

It is a natural tendency for parents to want the best for their daughters. However, this may backfire on some parents when a rebellious daughter brings up the point that her father was not a doctor or a lawyer and yet was a father and a husband to the family. Or her father may be a deadbeat dad who is not mindful of his family, which would put the mother in a position of an unqualified judge in the current situation for her daughter. This is a perfect example to show that it is not what a man does that makes him a man; it is who he is on the inside as a person that matters. She may love her dad regardless of his occupation and value his input as a parent. I cannot help but imagine what Grandma on the mother's side thought about her dad being a band drummer back in the days when he met her mom. But let us leave good old Grandma out of the picture and there is nothing wrong with being a band drummer.

The other alternative is that the mother may like him, but the daughter is undecided. A mother's input may influence her daughter's decision not to choose him as her soul mate. Her daughter's decision is based on her independence of choice rather than being coerced by her mom. The only way her mother's input is of value is when her daughter has already made her choice in agreement with her. Her mother's perception may also be painting a picture of being too old-fashioned. It is like saying that if your mother likes him, then he may not be a good fit.

With the generation gap becoming smaller, this problem seems to be fading as mothers and daughters are closer in age, wearing the same clothes, listening to the same music, going to the same clubs, and attending the same concerts. Younger single mothers are more concerned if the guy is cute enough to be seen with their daughters—or in some cases whether he has an older brother. You may even find a daughter calling her mom to pick her up from a club and only to find out that her mom is at the same club but on a different floor, where alcohol is served.

The process of asking for parental approval in most cases is superficial at best and is mostly done out of respect. The bride and groom-to-be will no doubt carry on with the wedding plans, and though the approval from parents may not be in full, nevertheless they should give blessings and well-wishes to the couple.

Chapter 16

Valentine's Day

It is that time of year again when bouquets of flowers are conveniently sold on street corners along with cute teddy bears. Card stores restock their inventory, and chocolate makers are in for their seasonal profits. Love is in the air, and you have only two days left to prepare for that special day stamped on the calendar. A day that is phony for most, who truly lack the real essence of romance but try with mundane attempts to justify its worth. The day that acts as an alarm clock reminding them that the chivalry of romance is very much alive.

It is understood that sometimes the monotony of life dampens the appreciation of a relationship, and this day is used to rekindle a burned-out flame, but in some cases, there is absolutely nothing to rekindle, so, trying to ignite a flame may lead to burning down the relationship completely. On other occasions, it is a sweet gesture to surprise an unsuspecting partner who may appreciate the romance of the day and does not feel left out.

For those who are in a long-distance relationship and hardly see each other, it can be quite a challenging experience. Meet Steve and Jasmin, who endured a long-distance relationship for years due to their professions. He was making good money with the family window installation business in Atlanta, Georgia, while she was working as a boutique store manager in Miami, Florida. They would text and call each other throughout the day to fill the void of not being together in person. They would see each other approximately once or twice every three months, and they would sometimes plan to be together on that special day of the year. She would visit him in Atlanta, or he would make the trip to Miami.

As time progressed, it became evident that the distance was taking its toll on the relationship, and the absence of a partner next to him or her regularly could not be replaced with texting, phone calls, and the occasional video chat. Her visits to him became fewer, and the calls and texting from her became infrequent. He would call but could not reach her as easily as before, and sometimes he had to leave a message. Steve sensed that his Jasmin may be slipping away from him like a cube of ice on an uneven surface. It became even more striking when, on his last visit to her, there was a strange and awkward silence that something was wrong. She assured him that all was fine and that she was just a bit depressed knowing that he would be traveling back home in a few days.

Steve thought about the situation and figured it was about time he made the sacrifice by moving to Florida to be with her. After all, they had endured a relatively long relationship without being in the same state. To heighten this surprise, he planned and choose Valentine's Day to present her with the usual box of chocolate, roses, a cute and cuddly teddy bear, and a personal Valentine's Day card he had created. He would then seal the deal with a marriage proposal and an engagement ring. Four days before his big presentation, he spoke with her to test the waters of her emotions. She acted a bit disappointed that he would not be present for Valentine's Day but assured him that she would be okay and would be cooking at home. Fate worked in Steve's favor that she would be off from work that day, Steve's heart was pounding, and he had a sense of exhilaration to go through with the surprise.

That fateful day on the calendar finally arrived, and Steve Face Timed her early in the morning. She was not fully awake, as she yawned, rubbed her eyes, and both indulged in pillow talk and sweet nothings for about an hour. Steve abruptly ended the conversation, saying he had a work appointment he had to fulfill, and then he hurriedly prepared himself for his Valentine's Day presentation. He called her again in a few hours while on his journey, but her phone went to voicemail, which for him was not unusual because she had stated that sometimes she would leave her phone at home while she walked her dog. Steve arrived at her home at about 5:30 p.m. that evening intending to complement the evening surprise with dinner at her favorite restaurant.

Upon arriving at her home, there was nothing peculiar—until he saw the look on her face as she curiously opened the door and saw him with arms filled with a box of chocolate, a bunch of flowers, and a stuffed bear. She awkwardly asked, "What are you doing here?" but quickly realized that may have been the wrong response. With her eyes wide open, she nervously glanced back over her shoulder into the living room, while she stood there being a bit hesitant. Her facial expression went from surprised to puzzle and confused with an awkward smile.

He then asked, "Are you going to invite me in?"

She clumsily answered, "Aah, sure."

Upon entering the living room, Steve could immediately sense that something was not quite right. There were way too many lit candles, and the room had a romantic setting. She had never prepared this type of setting for him in all his prior visits, and it would have been great if she were expecting him—but this was not a welcoming site for Steve.

If a woman wants to set a mood by herself, then who am I to judge? But I truly cannot imagine any man at this point thinking that all was well as it became even more suspicious when Steve saw boxes of chocolate on a table with a huge vase of fourteen red roses. A big red and white teddy bear, twice the size as the one he held in his hands, sat on the couch staring in his direction while dressed in a tie that said, "I love you."

Steve then heard a running faucet in the bathroom down the hall and the shuffling around of someone behind a closed bathroom door. Jasmin stuttered, "My-my friend is here." Steve's heart sank as he now braced himself to see who was about to exit the bathroom to replace him. How could she do this to him? The door slowly opened to reveal a young, attractive woman exiting the bathroom wearing a sexy red laced lingerie. Jasmin then quickly said, "Megan, this is Steve. Steve, meet Megan." Megan quickly recognized the situation and calmly said, "Hi", then made a quiet retreat to Jasmin's bedroom and closed the door. Jasmin awkwardly ran both hands through her hair and took a deep breath, looked at Steve, and then said, "We need to talk."

Some freaky men would not be too disappointed when she said, "We need to talk," hoping that she would be including them in a threesome. But for Steve, that was not the case. It was not only a shocker for him but also an awkward experience—and the end of his relationship. He will never view Valentine's Day the same because this incident will always be a reminder. Did he wait too long to make his move, or was it the long-distance relationship that finally did him in? Was she bi-curious? If it was not for Valentine's Day, Steve may have been in a relationship that was heading for an inevitable end. The actions on Valentine's Day sometimes reflect what is happening below the surface in a person's life. For most women in a relationship, the day acts as a thermometer of their closeness, and many times guys are kicked to the curb for not recognizing its importance. Some women and men do not care whether the actions are fake or genuine; they will still appreciate the effort.

The act of wishing someone a happy Valentine's Day has extended to everyone, and whether in a relationship or not, the gesture of giving a simple gift has become the accepted norm for many.

In closing, there are three distinct categories each person will be in on February 14. The first is doing something extra for and with that person you have developed a relationship within your life. The second is doing something romantic for or with someone you have not done anything with in your life. The third and last, which many of us may not want to admit, serves as a dreaded yearly reminder that there is absolutely nothing romantic going on in our lives.

Chapter 17

Cold Feet Before Marriage

"The Bride Who Ran Away." Yes! You read it correctly: The bride who ran away. Most women relish the idea of being married; after all, the bride will be the star of the day, and all the glory and attention will rightfully be on her. I also believe she gave a favorable response to his request while he was down on a bent knee. Therefore, it would be unlikely of her to opt-out of such a glorious event. But first, let us turn the tables and let me tell you the story about Carl, a young man who was supposed to get married on a Saturday but disappeared on the Thursday before his wedding.

Carl worked in the family business and owned a farm approximately ten acres in size. This land also accommodated a small farmhouse that was situated some twenty minutes away from his home. It was unknown to many but customary for him to park inside the farmhouse and lock himself in behind a tall wooden door. It so happened that while working in his farmhouse, some hardware from a top-shelf fell on him, knocking him unconscious to the ground. On regaining consciousness, he realized that not only was he injured, but he was pinned to the floor and could not remove some of the heavy plywood resting on his leg. He tried shouting for help, but his attempts were useless because there was no one within distance to hear him.

His fiancée thought she had scared him away once she mentioned how many children she wanted to have. Carl was reported missing, but the local law enforcement officers refused to search in the belief that he had skipped town. Jovan, his older brother, knew Carl was not afraid of the commitment of marriage and that he was looking forward to Tying the Knot with the love of his life. The search party for Carl consisted of his fiancée, Jovan, his dad, and his dog. Not many genuinely cared because they thought he had skipped town to escape the commitment of marriage.

Fortunately, Carl was found on the day that was supposed to be his wedding day. The wedding was postponed until the following Saturday, and Carl walked down the isles on crutches. You most likely will never hear the story of Carl simply because it is not newsworthy, and the thought of his wife killing him and hiding his body would somehow seem illogical.

We rarely hear the story of the guy who goes out to buy a pack of cigars days before his wedding and never shows up again, presuming he is as scared as a raccoon at the consequences he might face as a married man for the rest of his life. Chances are, no one would be looking for his sorry scared butt. Nobody cares, and probably only his mother, his fiancée, his father, and his faithful pet dog would be a bit concerned about his whereabouts. He could have very well been kidnapped or even killed, but to disappear a few days before his wedding would not warrant a search. A missing cat or dog would have had the whole community searching.

In this instance where the tables are turned; it did happen, and she left him before going to the altar. The groom thought he knew his bride, but much to his embarrassment, he did not.

Many believe that the majestic late entrance of the bride while the groom patiently waits at least an hour is because she must appear perfect for him, and it does take a while for her to put on her gown and ensure her makeup is flawless as she makes a grand entry. The wedding guests are also waiting to see her and her wedding gown in all its glory. Furthermore, a man waiting on his bride shows an outward reflection and token of his love. They did say that "Good things come to those who wait." But the real reason for his wait is hidden under the presentation. He is not trusted under any circumstances to have her do the waiting. Having her wait, along with the wedding guests, may eventually lead to a wedding not being performed that day—or worse yet, called off. He may decide to change his mind and have the guests and his lovely decked-out bride waiting for him while he slips out of his attire after having second thoughts. Everyone trusts the bride, but no one seems to trust the groom. Now you know why a best man is necessary. He is there to make sure the groom does not jump ship. Regardless of what his duties entail on paper, the underlining reasons are there. The best-woman was then included but obviously for different reasons.

The irony of a man opting out is rare since he initiated the union upon his request, and she accepted.

Having cold feet or jitters before a wedding is a natural occurrence. But the extent of this jitter should not be in the form of running away. Her family and friends are worried, not knowing her whereabouts. The groom-to-be is interrogated by cops. Women nationwide are blaming him for abuse. The media is camping out at his house with the anticipation of searchers finding a body. The cops are doing a futile search for absolutely nothing at taxpayers' expense, only to find out it was all a hoax as she resurfaces with a cooked-up false story of being kidnapped. It does not take much to figure out that her issues may be far more problematic than getting cold feet before marriage. For this drama to be finalized and a marriage knot tied, it is evident that someone else takes her role other than the Runaway Bride for the starring role in this saga.

A bride running off on the wedding day is extremely rare. There are many options for her to consider before drastically running away. She could have easily confided in her fiancé. After all, she did say yes to his proposal while he was on bent knees. If not him, then she could have confided in her family. This story could also be in the "Makes no Sense" category. There is an excuse and consideration for someone not proceeding with a wedding, but there is no excuse for how the runaway bride did it. Who knows? Probably there were not enough people on the guest list, so she had to include a nation. Let us hope for his sake he chose to postpone until further notice.

Chapter 18

The Wedding Before, During and After

A day dreaded by some, appreciated by few, and celebrated by all. Yes! That day finally arrives when they say, "I do," but let us keep that thought on hold for a while longer.

Does she know what she is looking for? Is she looking for the right thing? Is she looking in the right places? Are men ready to commit? Does he know what he really wants? Do they both have the right approach to being married? Some believe it is a necessary accomplishment at a certain stage of their lives, while some see it as a status symbol. For others, it is peer pressure among friends. Some may even see it as a more legit way to have kids based upon their family values and acceptance. Whatever the reasons, it should never be rushed or forced, and it is not a crime if you are single. Too often people rush into this process without clearly thinking it through, which leads to an early exit. Remember, you might not get exactly what you are looking for, but at least you would be happy and content as your love grows and blossoms under the lasting bond and appreciation for your partner rather than subside over time due to lack of commitment. Oops! I think I hear the bells ringing … Okay, let us get back to the wedding.

Marriage was meant to be a lasting union between a man and

a woman. The actual wedding day, the highlight to celebrate this unification. The man has finally thrown up the white flag and surrendered himself to this merger. Most of his friends are married, and he does not want to become the oddball in his group or become a regular fixture at the bar or strip club gawking at the ass of some young dancer every week. For the woman, she may view marriage as a status in life. Whether this is true or not depends on her mindset and how she plans on displaying the rock on her finger.

The special day is etched in stone approximately a year before the big event, and every day seems like a great countdown to this gala. The setting for the bride is like a true fantasy. Family, close friends, and acquaintances are notified of this event on stylish glossy cards that make all guests have a sense of grand importance about this special occasion. All her energy is focused and wrapped up in preparation for the grand festivity. She ultimately greenlights and approves all plans for this fairyland drama, with the groom occasionally putting in his two cents. She wants a garden of roses, a stylish snow-white wedding gown, a fleet of bridesmaids with matching groomsmen, family and dearest friends, video and photography, a huge cathedral decorated with aisles of flowing red and white arches, red carpet, a white horse and carriage, a four-tier cake, an ever-flowing fountain of wine, a live band, gifts galore, and surprises. Then there is a continuation in his and her chosen paradise in the picturesque beaches of Tahiti or the Maldives on a one-week honeymoon. Wow! I am out of breath. Some settings might not be so elaborate, but it is a moment for her and her partner to indulge.

She is ready to star in her movie, with the groom being her best supporting male actor. The day finally arrives, and every event is on cue, which translates to running late. The day seems like forever as they both are overwhelmed with planned activities crammed into half a day.

The Hollywood settings on that perfect day lead to high expectations after this fairy tale paradise has ended. The smiles, laughter, and cheers along with the picture-perfect images on photo and film are etched in memory as a constant reminder of this heavenly atmosphere.

Soon the deacon has extended his farewell, guests and wedding participants are gone, the church decorations are taken down, the red carpet is rolled up and placed back in storage, the video and photography guys have left, the reception hall is empty, the band has packed up their stuff, the food is finished, and the wine glasses are empty with lipstick stains being the only evidence. There are no more bottles left with a cork, and the staff cleaners are busily clearing up for the next event.

Once this experience has ended and the credits begin to roll, then the true reality of life kicks into gear. Sometimes this fairy tale drama ends abruptly within the honeymoon setting as the backdrop now reads, "Trouble in Paradise." Somehow the "for worse" portion of the vows is conveniently forgotten. This extends into the ups and downs of life, with the latter being more frequent, and eventually takes its toll. The thought of going through life with this "I do" person tends to lose its meaning, and unforeseen issues that were quietly swept under the rug or were not in focus now raise their ugly heads. She now cries divorce as soon as the union becomes sour. She cries for divorce as soon as there is a conflict. She cries divorce when she realizes that this union may very well be for sickness, for worse, and for poorer. She must now escape the wrath of "till death do us part" and set herself free from this major blunder, possibly blaming Mom and Dad who simultaneously cleared their throats when the deacon asked, "If there is anyone present who has just cause why this couple should not be united let them speak now or forever hold their peace." The requested song played at the wedding now serves as a reminder of the beginning of sorrow. The diamond ring costing him a fortune, which he faithfully charged to his credit card, has now become an unfaithful, pricey symbol that maintains its monetary worth but lacks sentimental value.

Statistics show fifty percent of marriages end in divorce, which easily but shockingly translates to one in every two, thereby proving the wedding day to be nothing more than a meaningless sequence of events. The man may see this as a golden opportunity to get back in the dating scene by default. For him, there may be unfinished business to take care of on the outside. The woman, now feeling scarred, will pick up the broken pieces and continue with her life.

Allow me to share a brief history of the origin of the engagement ring and diamond ring. In 860 AD, Pope Nicholas decreed that an engagement ring become a required statement of nuptial intent. He insisted that these rings be made of gold, which signified a financial sacrifice on the part of the prospective husband. The diamond ring originated with King Maximillian, who presented Mary of Burgundy with a diamond ring in 1477 as a token of his love. The Venetians popularized the custom during the fifteenth century. The diamond was the hardest and most enduring substance in nature, so it followed that the engagement and marriage would endure forever.

It may seem unfair to compare the endurance of a natural stone to the unpredictability of humans. With the high divorce rate and the volatility of both partners, it would be safe to say a Cubic Zirconia would represent the union until a real sense of commitment and love is established between couples before the purchase of a diamond ring. Once this drama known as divorce is played out in the most brutal way of verbal and physical mudslinging, hate, and assets grabbing, the dust clears, and both genders are left to pick up the pieces and carry on with their lives. For some, this may be a burden financially, and for others, it may be a financial gain. A woman worries about the future -- until she gets a husband. A man never worries about the future -- until he gets a wife.

Some relationships are not even worth the plastic ring purchased from a vending machine for a quarter. Too often couples get married with totally different agendas in mind.

For many, the problem often arises through a lack of communication, which then leads to a lack of shared vision. This may also lead to spiritual and emotional disconnect. If the foundation of the relationship was based on the love of money as its priority, then financial stress will poison other areas of the relationship. It is a proven fact that money is the root of most marriage failures. The only time the relationship may seem good is a few minutes before bedtime, and that ends in the shake of a lamb's tail. After a while, everything becomes repetitive, and sparkles and flames that were ignited in the initial stages now refuse to rekindle.

Though the intentions of the merger may be in good faith of a brighter future together, we often find the first intention of the union, especially in younger adults, was to make living conditions easier on both. The *"I pay a portion and you pay a portion"* is adopted. This mentality then leads to the lessening of one's self-worth in a relationship. The notion that the union was formed mainly, for this reason, has caused men and women to put fifty percent of themselves in the merger rather than a whole. I am not saying that it cannot work, but the woman might find it necessary to spend two thousand dollars on cute designer jeans or a pocketbook. The husband may then find it necessary to equal his wife's spending habits. He may buy himself a bunch of unnecessary car accessories or overindulge in an expensive (maybe hidden) hobby. All this is done while neither is earning enough money to truly afford their desires. I agree that both should have their respective interests and individuality. They are also free to spend as they wish. However, the examples used often lead to self-indulgent rather than communal thoughts. There must be a balance. Both parties should try to make themselves efficient in taking charge in full at any given time, whether out of shared love or consideration to a given situation. It is understood that one might choose to go left while the other goes right. The problem is when one goes too far left while the other goes too far right, and both lose track of the base. Often the mindset of the individuals is self-governing and about to their survival, not the union.

The other scenario that may occur is that the husband or wife may be making more money and is expected to take care of the larger household bills. A man is more likely to compromise with his wife if he is the one bringing home the bacon. He is more likely to leave it up to her to make certain decisions at home. If the wife is making more money, the husband does not have a word other than "Yes dear" in any decision-making. The couch in the living room may very well be pink and blue, and the drapes may be orange and red. He must now pretend that it is quite fashionable. Her title is now changed from wife to woman of the house, and the husband's title of man of the house seems to be defined only by his gender. The husband will agree outwardly with certain decisions made for the sake of signing the contract of this merger, but he inwardly disagrees. If husband and wife agree on every issue without compromising on any of them, then chances are somebody is being a hypocrite.

For those that are financially secure; the sharing of quality time and interest may also become extremely rare as both are caught up with their complexities of life. If they fail to arrange a special time together, then the relationship becomes dull. Everything becomes the run-of-the-mill, and communication becomes less. A child coming into the equation after the husband has spilled his beans makes this relationship, which may now be hopping on one leg, an even harder task. In some cases, the child acts as a cushion between the two and serves as a valid distraction. Sooner or later, the term "irreconcilable differences" floats into existence and serves as a reasonable exit strategy. The vows exchanged on that perfect day seem progressively harder to swallow.

The strong women who faithfully stand in marriage and tolerate the unforeseen issues presented by men should be commended for staying the course for the sake of the union and their children. However, there are a handful of women who view marriage as an opportunity in life rather than a journey, with the sole intention of running with half of whatever they can grab once the timing is right for the killing, calling it quits after the first bump in the road.

Here is where honesty plays an exceptionally important part in a relationship. The comfort of knowing to trust your partner's actions and words will no doubt lead to a healthy, long-lasting relationship. The thought of cheating may also surface in the minds of some couples but carrying through with the thought of cheating will poison the relationship, though this action may awkwardly seem to justify itself in the minds of couples who are in a relationship that is on the road to destruction.

The final story I am going to share is about Philip and Tamara, a Californian couple who had been married for eight years—which incidentally is the average timeline for marriage. They got married after dating for two years, but unfortunately, the union did not produce any kids due to her having a miscarriage. Nevertheless, this brought them closer together. Philip was immensely popular in his high school and college years. He was very athletic, participated in every sport, and was a natural charmer of the ladies. He dated all the alpha women back in college, and it did not bother them that he was not fully committed to any of them. His swing with the ladies continued well beyond his college years, and at one point he was dating a beauty contestant who represented the state. His college yearbook described him as the prince who would be least likely to have a princess.

When he finally decided to settle and marry Tamara at the age of twenty-eight, it was a surprise to many of his friends who knew of his past. It appeared that he had truly found the love of his life and a woman who would eventually tame his former lifestyle. The wedding day was not as elaborate as the one stated earlier, but in all, it was a moment for them to cherish.

She was devoted to him and making a family. After renting an apartment for a few years, they decided to purchase a home and made it their love nest. Then one evening on his way home from work, she called him to pick up a box of milk and bread from their local supermarket. He knew that by the time he would have gotten there, it would have been closed, so he instead stopped at a closer marketplace in his immediate locale. Upon arriving, he went straight for the box of milk and then headed for the bread aisle. A female voice within hearing distance said, "Philip, is that you?" He looked toward the produce section and saw a young miss sporting tight blue jeans and a white top holding a small shopping basket in her left hand.

"Hi," he said awkwardly, not knowing who it was.

She immediately realized that he did not recognize her. "Sharon, from the Acting Studio Club?" she blurted out. Only then did he remember he had dated a few women; all of whom were attending the same acting school to get their big break in showbiz.

"Hey! It has been a while. How did things work out for you?" he asked.

"Not too good," she replied. "I decided to eventually give up and move on." She paused a few seconds and continued. "I ended up being a waitress at the downtown eatery before I formed my own business."

"Great, that's the way to go—be in charge of your destiny," Philip replied. He then noticed an engagement ring on her finger. "So, who is the lucky guy in your life?"

"That didn't work out too well either, so now I am happily single."

At this juncture, Philip knew he had to let her know he was happily married. He instead downplayed it by saying, "I got hooked by a bait a few years ago."

She shrewdly said, "Good for you, good for you. I can imagine she is a lucky woman." She had a playful grin. They continued to chat for another five minutes, and with each passing moment, she whipped her long hair out of her face while occasionally touching his arms and shoulders to emphasize a point.

The conversation came to an end as he glanced at his watch and said, "I've got to run now."

She said, "Oh, I am so sorry I took up your time. I have not spoken to anyone much like this since I have broken up with my ex." She then gave him a quick hug, turned away, and headed for the checkout. She wore high-heeled shoes that accentuated her calves, and her buns were perfectly round in her jeans as she firmly took each step with confidence. Philip stood there and watched as she walked with a sense of poise while holding her head high and her chest out.

As he slowly walked off, he reasoned with himself. "What harm would be to just take her number? Knowing that she would gladly let him have the digits, he caught up with her and said, "Let me have your number. I have a good friend you would love to meet."

She smiled and jokingly said, "As long as it's not your wife then I am okay."

He smiled back and said, "No."

It so happened that she did not meet that friend he was referring to, but that was okay by her because she would instead see Philip regularly when the time was convenient for both. Philip knew in his heart that he was being unfaithful to Tamara, but the urge of attraction for Sharon revealed the old Philip. He felt like a runaway train going downhill, unable to apply brakes. She certainly did not make it easy on him because he was a breath of fresh air for her in a vulnerable situation. She got the attention and emotional support she so desperately craves. It would only be a matter of time before he got caught up in her grasp and eventually succumbed to the sugar mine between her legs. Like an addict on crack, he kept going back for more while knowing that he was being unfaithful to Tamara.

He soon began sinking into depression as the feeling of guilt started to override his conscience. He genuinely loved his wife and did not want to hurt her in any way. Sometimes he wondered if she was aware of the feminine scent of perfumes on his clothing, but she seemed not to suspect any foul play. He always made an excuse for coming home late or going somewhere abruptly, but often she would dismiss it as nothing because she too was taken up in her regular book club meetings at her girlfriend's home. Most nights after they had dinner, he would be too tired and lack the stamina to make out with Tamara, and often he would leave her unsatisfied by drifting off in a snore.

He finally came to terms that the selfish disloyalty he displayed must come to an end to save his marriage. He realized that it would have been difficult for him to make an admission to her, but he also came to terms with the fact that he needed help. He decided to join an organization that helped cheating spouses. He found one that was far enough from his community and attended.

After finishing up work at the office, he drove a couple of miles and found the venue. It was held in an auditorium of a small church. The parking lot was full, but he was able to find a spot and hastily head toward a sign on a door saying in capital letters, "CAG." The meeting had already started, so he gently pushed the door open and noticed that there were not any more chairs left to be seated. He joined the rest of the people standing at the back next to the entry door. Upfront was a stocky bearded man sporting a pair of glasses with a strong, sturdy voice that filled the room. Seated next to him was a woman with heavy makeup on her face who may have been a man but had changed gender; the giveaway was the appearance of Adam's apple in her throat. The meeting went on for a few minutes until Philip recognized a familiar figure from behind in the front row. He slowly walked to the side of the room to get a better view. To his surprise and dismay, it was Tamara. He was shocked. He gently walked back toward the rear of the room, trying not to bring much attention to himself.

As he steadily made his way for the exit, the bearded man suddenly uttered, *"Sir, please don't leave. You came for a purpose. Let us fulfill that purpose."* Philip did not break his stride but quickly exited the room. Did their marriage survive? Did she saw him leaving? What was she doing there? Was she also cheating? Was she there to get help as a victim of a cheater? Did they reconcile? I will keep you posted.

Your wishful answers to those questions will determine whether you are an optimist or pessimist, man or woman, along with your own experiences in life and perspective. It does appear that they are at the right place to get help. However, being secretive about their actions to save their marriage ironically backfires for both. If they had come clean about their actions, as burdensome as it may seem, it would have been easier for them. Honesty, loyalty, and communication were missing in action. These qualities are essential, and if they go, the building blocks of love in his marriage will come crashing down. You do not have to be a marriage counselor to understand that marriage is a lasting union shared in mutual interest and communication on all levels. Nowadays, couples are increasingly seeing marriage as a destination rather than a shared journey over a rocky or smooth pavement. The valleys may be okay, but the hills may cause a problem, therefore, the beauty of marriage is not defined in the sharing of good times, but the overcoming of obstacles as a union. The thought of separation should be the last thing on anyone's mind and not the first. Divorce attorneys do not have to wait for a knock on their doors or a ring on their phones to get in on a piece of the action. A divorce, especially if brutal, is the fastest way not to get rich for many, and it is a luxury only the wealthy can afford. The emotional and psychological impact may also linger on, months and years after a divorce. The whole process of marriage and divorce may have purposely been for conniving reasons to an unsuspecting partner that has hung up their former lifestyle of tired of being alone, thinking that they have found the true love of their life.

I started this topic on a bright note on that wedding day, so let us end it the same. The wedding day, picture-perfect setting, exchanges of vows and rings, signing of the certificate, and captured images of the moment are simply a symbolic footprint in the sands that will eventually play itself out in time. A love between a man and a woman is a beautiful thing. A marriage is a consecration of that love, a legal binding of vows for each other. There is only one wedding day, but a marriage will have days, weeks, months, and years of sharing life with that special someone. If thoughts were genuine when exchanging vows, then the marriage will last and even exceed expectations of well-wishers, thereby proving it to be the rightful definition of love.

Chapter 19

The Wrap-Up

The wrap-up is where I wind things down as we approach the end. Within the contents of this book, you may have smiled, laughed, expressed sorrow, pondered on some issues, or even found things offensive. It all depends on your perspective on life. Many of these issues may not frequently flow to our awareness, but when they do, they act as a mirror to our souls, therefore it is my hope and wishes that you take something positive from this book and do not dwell on the negative.

Men And women; said to be from Mars and Venus respectively, living together on planet earth. *Untold Stories, Him and Her* highlights the issues that face both genders being vulnerable to each other. This vulnerability has us exposing our emotions with the hope of goodwill. The actions that distinguish us as male or female, are influenced by the opposite sex. If you were in doubt, then this book should clear that up.

In closing, allow me to state that sometimes we need to rediscover and reevaluate our inner selves. A house becomes a home when we personalize its interior to our taste and style. We become better than what our image portrays when our actions are genuine from the heart. In the journey of life, men and women will meet at the intersections, and whether they choose to stop and obey the signals or ignore them and cause a collision is their decision. They can be the best of friends, be worst enemies, or play each other. The exhilarating experience of getting to know each other with great expectations for the future depends on everyone's perceptions. Unfortunately, that perception is not the same for everyone.

A few words associated with a great relationship are loyalty, respect, fairness, endurance, trust, harmony, acceptance, humility, empathy, content, growth, selflessness, and I could go on forever. But the defining word that all these words are packed into is that simple four-letter word called love. Love not only for others but also for ourselves. The word love can be related to every topic in this book.

However! In keeping within the usual trends of this book, I must admit the obvious truth. For most of us, the reality of applying those words to our lives is like grasping a wet soap that keeps slipping from the palms of our hands. The truth is that we possess natural imperfections as human beings, making those charming words easier written or said than being done. On that note, many more untold stories will emerge. Take care until next time.

Author's Notes

The premise of this book is based on my love for the arts and literature, combined with storytelling. I believe art is an imitation of life, expressed on paper, film, or any surface. We can tell a story, make an illustration, or share a viewpoint through drawings, photos, motion pictures, or writing. The contents of this book were created from the blueprint of various opinions and combined experiences. The driving motivation to put pen to paper was to share those experiences, not only in a story setting but also in a general opinionated approach. Though the topics are highly dogmatic, are also subjected to open debates. *Untold Stories, Him and Her,* is intended to be enlightening, engaging, funny, heartbreaking, and thought-provoking.

The major challenge in writing this book was to be forthright about relationship issues and present them as a balance between him and her. We naturally experience life through various lenses that act as our unique viewpoints. Therefore, I hope that the subject matters expressed in this book are not assumed literally.

Q&A with Author Wayne Dean

Q: What prompted me to write this book?

A: Various things prompted me to write, but I believe the most important one was just an eagerness to share the experience. I would have loved to do short movies to relay these stories in narration but lack the resources. A book was my natural next option due to my love for writing.

Q: Why named it "Untold Stories, Him and Her?"

A: The original title, when I started, was "Women, Men, and Untold Stories". There was also a different cover. I changed it because women and men sounded a bit too against each other. "Him and Her" gave it a sense of both being involved, though the book was written from a male perspective. "Untold stories" are things we rarely discuss.

Q: How long did it take me to write?

A: Interestingly, this project started approximately eight years ago, and was sitting on the shelves for some time. I decided to take it off the shelf, dust it off, made changes, added more, and take out chapters. It took approximately five months to complete.

Q: Why do I exclude chapters?

A: As raw as the book is now, there were chapters I believe were a bit too sensitive or chapters I believe would not connect well with readers in general.

Q: Is there any person in my life that I can easily relate to the circumstances in the book?

A: When drafting the book, I do not think of anyone I would use as an example in my life. All examples are generalized; therefore, any relatable situation is purely coincidental.

Q: Is the book based on my opinion?

A: It is a general opinion shared through the eyes of various sources including me. My work was to justify those opinions and present them as facts. Though my overall intent was also focused on evoking emotion as in most storytelling rather than an actual true story.

Q: Am I aware that some people will not agree or share the same opinions?

A: That is natural and an expected reaction. The book is highly debatable and may naturally stir discussion. The intent of the book was not done for all to agree in unison. I leave that to books dealing with self-help and spirituality and even with those books, you will find disagreements.

Q: Who are my targeted readers?

A: Actually, anyone who is not thin-skinned and can read a book without letting the book rock their boat into negativity. My targeted readers are young adults, middle-agers, and the elderly, the latter who may also relate to when they were younger or currently dealing with an adult son or daughter. The book's purpose is to read, hopefully, find it interesting, talk about it with friends, then get on with life.

Q: Are there any parts of the book or chapter that I feel are defining the book or sent an overall message to readers?

A: This may be a spoiler for those who have not read the book yet, but the very last chapter sums up the book, and the last paragraph pretty much sums up everyone reading it.

Q: What would I say is most appealing about this book?

A: I tried to make it as descriptive and engaging as possible while allowing the reader to ride along with me using their imagination. Real-life scenarios are used with the reader narrating the whole book while picturing each situation. Each chapter is completed on a positive note so as not to leave the reader in a negative state.

Q: Will I be doing any relationship speeches in the future or participating in any related discussions?

A: I do not want to be identified as a relationship guru. I leave that to the experts. There is no greater teacher than life itself. The book has a greater percentage of entertainment value overall and should not be used as a guide in any relationship. The expressed views were done from a basic perspective and does not delve into the mechanism of how a relationship should prosper.

Printed in the United States
by Baker & Taylor Publisher Services